IN
OTHER
WORLDS

A. A. Attanasio

BANTAM BOOKS

TORONTO • NEW YORK • LONDON • SYDNEY • AUCKLAND

IN OTHER WORLDS
*A Bantam Spectra Book / published by arrangement with
William Morrow & Co., Inc.*

PRINTING HISTORY
*Morrow edition published January 1985
Bantam edition / March 1986*

*My thanks to Rick Buitz for permission to use his composition
Evoë, page 65*

ISBN 0-553-25566-5

Published simultaneously in the United States and Canada

PRINTED IN THE UNITED STATES OF AMERICA

O   0 9 8 7 6 5 4 3 2 1

You know who you are,
so this is for you.

Contents

He who looks does not find,
but he who does not look is found.

—KAFKA

IN
OTHER
WORLDS

Carl Schirmer's last day as a human was filled with portents of his strange life to come. As he completed his morning ablutions, he saw in the bathroom mirror his hair, what little of it there was, standing straight up. He smoothed it back and tucked it behind his ears with his damp hands, but it sprang back. Even the few strands left at the cope of his shining pate wavered upright. His hair was a rusty gossamer, and it stuck out from the sides of his large head like a clown's wig.

With his usual complaisance, he shrugged and commenced to shave his broad face. Today, he sensed, was going to be an unusual day. His sleep had been fitful, and he had awoken to a breed of headache he had never encountered before. His head was not actually aching—it was buzzing, as though overnight a swarm of gnats had molted to maturity in the folds of his brain. After completing his morning cleansing ritual and checking the coat of his tongue and the blood-brightness under his lids, he put his glasses on, took two acetaminophen, and dressed for work.

Carl was not a stylish or a careful dresser, yet even he noticed that his clothes, which he had ironed two nights before for a dinner his date had canceled and which had looked fine hanging in his closet, hung

1

particularly rumpled on him that day. When he tried to brush the wrinkles out, static sparked along his fingers. The morning was already old, so he didn't bother to change. He hurried through breakfast despite the fact that his usually trustworthy toaster charred his toast, and he skipped his coffee when he saw that no amount of wire-jiggling was going to get his electric percolator to work. Not until he had left his apartment and had jogged down the four floors to the street did he realize that his headbuzz had tingled through the cords of his neck and into his shoulders. He was not feeling right at all, and yet in another sense, a perceptive and ease-ful sense, he was feeling sharper than ever.

Carl lived in a low-rent apartment building on West Twenty-fourth Street and Tenth Avenue in Manhattan, and he was not used to smelling the river, though he was only a few blocks away from the Hudson. This morning the air for him was kelpy with the sweet-and-sour smell of the Hudson. Immense cauliflower clouds bunched over the city, and the blue of the sky seemed clear as an idea.

He strolled down Twenty-third Street with an atypically loose stride, his face uplifted to the path of heaven. Spring's promise-haunted presence drifted through the tumult of clouds, which was odd, since this was November. The rainbow-haired punks that loitered about the Chelsea Hotel looked childbright and friendly today, and Carl knew then that the ferment of a mood was indeed altering him. But he didn't care. Though his blood felt carbonated, it was wondrous to see the city looking benevolent, and he went with the illusion.

At the corner of Seventh Avenue, a drunk approached him, and he handed over a dollar, appreciating the serene desuetude of the woman's face. Nothing could depress him this morning. And the sight of the place where he worked sparked a smile in him. The Blue

Apple at Twenty-second and Seventh was a bar and restaurant that he managed. Except for the neon sign in the vine-trellised window, the structure was antiquated and looked smoky with age. Until Carl had come along, the narrow building had been an Irish bar with the inspired name the Shamrock, run and owned by Caitlin Sweeney, an alcoholic widow supporting her thirst and a daughter with the faithful patronage of a few aged locals. A year ago, after losing his midtown brokerage job to the recession and his own lack of aggression, Carl had let a newspaper ad lead him here. He had been looking for something to keep him alive and not too busy. And then he had met Sheelagh and wound up working harder than ever.

Caitlin's daughter had been sixteen then, tall and lean-limbed, with green, youthless eyes and a lispy smile. Carl was twice her age, and he lost his heart to her that first day, which was no common event with him. He had experienced his share of crooked romance and casual affairs in college, and for the last ten years he had lived alone out of choice sprung from disappointment. No woman whom he had found attractive had ever found him likewise. He was gangly, nearsighted, and bald, not ugly but lumpy-featured and devoid of the conversational charm that sometimes redeemed men of his mien. So instead of contenting himself with the love of a good but not quite striking woman, he had lived alone and close to his indulgences: an occasional spleef of marijuana, a semiannual cocaine binge, and a sizable pornography collection stretching back through the kinky Seventies to the body-painting orgies of the Sixties. Sheelagh made all the years of his aloneness seem worthwhile, for she was indeed striking—a tall, lyrical body with auburn tresses that fell to the roundness of her loose hips—and, most exciting of all, she needed him.

When Carl had arrived, the Shamrock was brinking on bankruptcy. He would never have had anything to do with a business as tattered as the one riven-faced Caitlin had revealed to him were Sheelagh not there. She was a smart kid, finishing high school a year ahead of her class and sharp enough with figures and deferred-payment planning to keep the Shamrock floating long after her besotted mother would have lost it. Sheelagh was the one, in her defiant-child's manner, who had shown him that the business could be saved. The neighborhood was growing with the artistic overflow from Greenwich Village, and there was hope, if they could find the money and the imagination, to draw a new, more affluent clientele. After talking with the girl, Carl had flared with ideas, and he had backed them up with the few thousand dollars he had saved. The debts were paid off, old Caitlin reluctantly became the house chef, and Carl took over the bartending, the books, and the refurbishing. A year later, the Shamrock had almost broken even as the Blue Apple, a name Carl had compressed from the Big Apple and the certain melancholy of his hopeless love for Sheelagh. That love had recently increased in both ardor and hopelessness now that Sheelagh had finished high school and had come to work full-time in the Blue Apple while she saved for college.

On Carl Schirmer's last day as a human, when he entered the restaurant with his collar of red hair sticking out from his head, his clothes knotted with static, and his eyes shining with the beauty of the day, Sheelagh was glad to see him. The new tables they had ordered had come in and were stacked around the bar, legs up like a bamboo forest. "Aren't they fine?" Sheelagh asked.

In the year since they had first met, she had filled out to the full dimensions of a woman, and Carl was not

4

addressing the tables when he answered: "Beautiful. Just beautiful."

With his help, she moved aside the old Formica-top table from the choice position beside the window and placed the new wooden one there. Sunlight smeared its top like warm butter. She sighed with satisfaction, turned to Carl, and put her arms about him in a jubilant hug. "It's happening, Carl. The Blue Apple is beginning to shine." She pulled back, startled. "You smell wonderful. What are you wearing?"

He sniffed his shoulder and caught the cool fragrance misting off him, a scent kindred to a mountain slope. "I don't know," he mumbled.

"Long night on the town, huh?" She smiled slyly. She truly liked Carl. He was the most honest man she'd ever known, a bald, boy-faced pal, soft around the middle but with a quiet heart and an inward certainty. His experience as an account exec had earned him managerial skills that to Sheelagh seemed a dazzling ease with the world of things. For the first year he ran the entire business on the phone, shuffling loans and debts until they burst into the black. He was a solid guy, yet he pulled no sexual feeling from her whatever. And for that reason, he had become in a short time closer to her than a brother. She had confided all her adolescent choices to him, and he had counseled her wisely through two high school romances and the lyric expectation of going to college someday. He knew her dreams, even her antic fantasy of a handsome, Persian-eyed lover. "From the looks of your clothes," she went on, "your date must have been quite an athlete." Her lubricious grin widened.

Carl pridefully buffed the thought with a smile and went about his business. The redolence of open space spun like magnetism about him all day, a day like most others: After getting the espresso machine and the

5

coffeemaker going at the bar, he brought the first hot cup to a hungover Caitlin in the kitchen.

The old woman looked as wasted as ever, her white hair tattering about her shoulders and her seamed face crumpled-looking from last night's drinking. Grief and bad luck had aged her more harshly than time, and she wore a perpetual scowl. But that morning when she saw Carl back through the swinging door of the kitchen, his hair feathering from his head and his clothes clinging like plastic wrap, a bemused grin hoisted her features. "Don't you look a sight, darlin'. Now, I know you don't drink, and you smell too pretty to have been rolled— so, mercy of God, it must be a woman! Do I know her?"

He placed the black coffee on the wooden counter before her, and she quaffed it though the brew was practically boiling in the cup. "It's not a woman, Caity."

"Ah, good, then there's still a chance for my Sheelagh" —she winked one liver-smoked eye—"when she's older and your hard work and bright ideas have made us all rich, of course."

Carl took down the inventory clipboard from its nail on the pantry door. "Sheelagh's too young and too smart to be interested in a bald coot like me."

"Ha! That's what you think. And she too probably. But you're both wrong." Caitlin sat back from her slump, refreshed by the steaming coffee. "Baldness is a sign of virility, you know. My Edward was bald, too. It's a distinguishing feature in a man. As for being too young, you're right. She's young with ideas of going off to college. But what's college for a woman? Just a place to meet a man."

"You know better than that, Caity," Carl told her as he prepared the reorder checklist. "Your daughter's smart enough to be anything she wants to be."

"And does she know what she wants to be? No. So why run off to college when she could be making her fortune here with a clever businessman like yourself? She should be thinking of the Sham—of the Blue Apple, and the lifetime her father gave to this place before the Lord called him and his weak liver answered. What's going to come of all this recent fortune and long hard work if she goes away? I'm not going to live forever."

"Not the way you drink, Caity. Have the ketchup and mayo we ordered gotten here yet?"

"They're in the cooler downstairs. I'm too old to stop drinking now, Carl. I haven't long to go. I can feel it. Old folk are that way. We know. But I'm not scared now that the Blue Apple has come around. Forty years Edward and I put into this tavern. And only the first ten were any good—but that was back when Chelsea was Irish. I would have sold out when it all changed after the war, but Edward had been brought up here, you know, and he had his dreams, like you have yours, only he wasn't near as handy at making them real. And then Sheelagh was born." She laughed, making a sound like radio noise. "I was forty-five when she was born. Is she God-sent or not, I ask you? Edward blamed the devil. No children for twenty-five years, and then a girl. I think that's what finally killed him, not the drink. If only he could have lived to meet you and see this: the house jammed every night—and eating my food, no less. Take off your glasses."

Carl peered over the rim of his wire glasses as he arranged the dry goods on the counter for that day's dinner menu.

"Why don't you get contact lenses?" Caitlin asked him. "Those glasses bend your face and make you look like a cartoon. And brush back your hair. If you're going to be bald, at least keep what you've got neat."

Carl was well acquainted with Caitlin's ramblings and admonitions, and he grinned away her jibes and checked the potato-and-leek soup she had prepared yesterday for this day's lunch. The old woman was an excellent cook. During the Forties she had worked as a sous chef in the Algonquin, and her dishes were savory and accomplished. She made all of the restaurant's fare with the help of a Chinese assistant who came in the afternoon for the dinner crowd. When Carl saw that the menu for the day was ready, he patted Caitlin on the shoulder and went out to set up the tables for lunch.

Caitlin Sweeney watched him go with a throb of heartbruise that the airy, springstrong scent he trailed only sharpened. She loved that man with a tenderness learned from a lifetime of hurting. She recognized the beauty in his gentleness that a younger woman like her daughter could only see as meekness. Like a lightning rod, Carl was strong in what he could draw to himself— as he had drawn more fortune to them in one year than her Edward for all his brawny good looks had drawn in forty years. Carl had the prize of luck only God could give. She saw that. And she saw, too, that Sheelagh, like herself in her hungry youth, yearned for the luckless arrogance of beauty. She sighed like the warmth of a dying fire leaking into the space-cold of night and put her attention on that day's cooking chores.

Carl was pleased that Caitlin encouraged his passion for Sheelagh, believing that the old woman was only teasing his interest in her daughter to keep him happy and hopeful. Carl's loneliness was the only lack Caitlin could pretend to complete in return for all he had done for them. Besides, Sheelagh was too self-willed for her mother's opinions to influence her even if the crone had really thought he was right for her. Carl spent little time pondering it that last day he lived as a man, for he was kept busy with his own strangeness.

Lightbulbs blinked out around him faster than he could replace them. And as he worked the bar for the afternoon business lunches, the reverie he had experienced that morning spaced out and became moony and distracted.

"You look pretty harried, sucker," a friendly, gravelly voice said as the blender he was trying to run for a banana daiquiri sputtered and stalled. He looked up into the swart-bearded face of Zeke Zhdarnov, his oldest friend. Zee was a free-lance science writer and part-time instructor of chemistry at NYU. He was a thickset man with a penchant for glenurquhart plaid suits and meerschaum pipes. Carl and Zee had been friends since their adolescence in a boys' home in Newark, New Jersey. They had nothing in common.

At St. Timothy's Boys' Home, Zee had been a husky, athletic ruffian and Carl a chubby, spectacled math demon. A mutual love for comic books brought them together and defied their differences. St. Tim's was a state house, and the place was haunted with dispirited, vicious youths from criminal homes. Zee offered protection from the roughs, and Carl did his best to carry Zee's classwork. At eighteen, Zee graduated to the Marines and Nam. Carl sought personal freedom by applying his math skills to finance at Rutgers University. A Manhattan brokerage drafted him straight out of the dorms. Meanwhile in Nam, Zee was learning all there was to know about the smallness of life. He paid for that education cheaply with the patella of his right knee, and he came back determined to invent a new life for himself. He studied science, wanting to understand something of the technology that had become his kennel. When that became too abstract, he went to work for a New Jersey drug company and married, wanting to find a feeling equal to the numbness that surrounded him. During his divorce, he had sought

9

out Carl, and the pain and rectification of that time had brought them together again, closer than they had ever been. Carl had done poorly at the brokerage, stultified by the anomie that had poisoned him from childhood but only oozed out of him after he had found enough security to stop his mad scramble from St. Tim's and catch the scent of himself. He had smelled sour, and not until he had met Sheelagh and developed the Blue Apple did he begin to feel good about himself. That was a year ago when Zee had reappeared. Now Zee came by often with a crowd of students to fill the Blue Apple up, and Carl was always happy to see him. They shook hands, and a loud spark snapped between their palms.

"Wow!" Zee yelled. "Are you charged! You look like you're being electrocuted—very slowly." He shifted his dark, slim eyes toward the table Sheelagh was clearing, her pendulous breasts swaying with her effort. "She's overloading you?"

"Today's an unusual day for me, buddy, but not that unusual. What'll you have?"

"Give me a Harp."

Carl took out a bottle of Harp lager from the ice cooler and poured it into a frosted mug. "The wiring's shot around the bar. I can't get this blender or even the damn lightbulbs to work right."

Zee reached over, and the blender purred under his touch. "It's the same way with women and me. The touch must be light yet assertive. I think you've got a lot of backed-up orgone in there." He stabbed Carl's midriff with a swizzle stick. "How about a run with me tomorrow? We'll follow the Westway down to the twin towers. I'll go easy on ya."

Carl agreed, and they chatted amiably about their usual subjects—slow running and fast women—while Carl tended to business. Later, as he was leaving, Zee leaned close and whispered: "No sense wearing that expensive cologne if you're going to dress like that." He reached out to shake, thought better of it, saluted, and left.

The rest of the day was a bumbling of small accidents for Carl. The bar's electrical system gave out entirely, and he had to mix drinks by hand and repeatedly go down to the basement cooler for ice. The tiny screws in his eyeglasses popped out, and he lost a lens down an open drain. Napkins clung tenaciously to his fingers, no matter how dry he kept them, and he spilled several drinks before he got used to the paper coasters coming away with his hand. Midway through the dinner shift, with the house jammed, the lights began dimming. When he left the bar to check the fuse box, the light came up, only to fade again on his return. "This is weird," Carl at last acknowledged, running both hands through his startled hair. Sparks crackled between his fingers. "I'm going home." He went over to the pay phone to call a neighborhood friend to cover for him, but he couldn't get a dial tone. Moments later a customer used the same phone without difficulty.

Carl waited until Sheelagh came to the bar with drink orders, then signed her toward a vacant corner. "What's wrong with me tonight, Sheelagh?"

"Your glasses are missing a lens. Your clothes need ironing. And you really should comb your hair."

"No—I mean, look at this." He touched her arm, and a large spark volted between them.

"Hey! Cut that out. That hurts."

"I can't stop it. I've been electrocuting customers all day. Look." He passed his hand over a stack of napkins, and the paper rose like drowsy leaves and clung to his fingers.

"It's some kind of static electricity," Sheelagh explained.

"I'll say. What can I do about it?"

"Keep your hands to yourself."

Spark surges thudded through him whenever he reached for metal, and after another hour of stiffening jolts, he sat on a stool at the far end of the bar and cradled his head in his hands.

"Is it that bad, darlin'?" A gentle hand touched his bald head, and another spark jumped.

Carl looked up into Caitlin's whiskey-bright eyes. A feeling of bloated peacefulness buoyed him at the sight of her time-snarled face. "Hi, Caity. Everything's wrong for me tonight. And I don't even know why."

"Just your luck taking a rest. Don't mind it. Have a drink."

"Nah—but I'd better get back to work."

"Wait." She took his hand, and another knot of electricity unraveled sharply with her touch. "I have to tell you." The marmalade-light in her stare dangled above him, and he could see the whiskey burning in her. "If only I *could* tell you what I've been humbled to. She doesn't know." She glanced toward where Sheelagh was serving a table, her sinewy elegance shining in the dim light. "You're a special man, Carl. Luck splits through you like light through a crystal. I see that. I see it because I'm old, and pain and mistakes have taught me how to see. You're a beautiful man, Carl Schirmer." Her scowl softened, and she turned away and went back to the kitchen. A customer called from the bar, and Carl rose like a lark into a smoky sunrise.

Caitlin's kind words fueled Carl for the rest of his last day, but by closing time he was feeling wrong again. He felt tingly as a glowworm, and all the tiny hairs on his body were standing straight up. He left Caitlin and Sheelagh to shut down the Blue Apple and walked home. An icy zero was widening in his chest, and he thought for sure he was going to be sick. Nonetheless, the beauty he had felt that morning was still there. Above the city lights, a chain of stars twined against the darkness, and the fabric of midnight shimmered like wet fur. Only the bizarre emptiness deepening inside him kept him from leaping with joy.

So self-absorbed was he with the bubble of vacancy expanding within him that he didn't notice the befuddled look on the face of the kid whose huge radio fuzzed out and in as Carl passed. Nor did he see the streetlights winking out above him and then flaring back brightly in his wake. The midnight traffic slowed to watch the neon lights in the stores along Twenty-third Street warble to darkness in his presence. Not until he had stumbled up the blacked-out stairs of his own building and had fumbled to get his key in the lock by the light of the sparks leaping from his fingers did he notice that a thin ghostfire was burning coolly over his hands and arms. He left the door unlocked behind him, afraid that something awful was happening to him. His apartment lights, like all the lights in the building, were browned out. The filaments in the bulbs glowed dark red but cast no radiance. The TV worked but gave no picture, only a prickly sound. He wheeled the TV to the door of the bathroom, and by its pulsing blue glow he had enough light to take a cold shower. The chilled water invigorated him, and when he looked down at his arms, he saw that the shimmering was gone, if it had been there at all. Relief widened in him, and he washed the one lens of his glasses and put them on to examine himself more closely.

The air was a vibration of luminance, and the wavering static of the TV seemed louder and more reverberant. He slid open the glass door to the shower, and his heart gulped panic. The TV was blacked out. The illumination and the sound were coming out of the air!

He jumped out of the shower stall and nearly collapsed. The bathroom was refulgent with frenzied light; waterdrops hung in the air like chips of crystal. Through the glare in the mirror, through an anvil of ripping-metal noise, he saw that his head was blazing with swirls of silvergreen flames. Dumbstruck, he watched the terror in his brilliantly oiled face as green fire fumed from his body in an incandescent rush.

A white-hot shriek cut through him, and his body went glassy, shot through with violet sparks and flurries of black light. Silence froze the room to a cube of crackling light. And the last thing Carl Schirmer saw was the glass of his own horrified face shatter into impossible colors.

Zee was the first to see Carl's apartment when he came by the next morning for their planned run. His knock went unanswered, but he heard the TV, so he tried the door. And it opened. The apartment smelled windshaken, bright as a mountaintop. Zee went over to the TV, which had been wheeled across the room to face the bathroom door and was blaring a morning soap. He turned it off.

"Oh sweet Jesus!" The words escaped him before he knew what he was seeing. The bathroom was a charred socket. The mirrors were purpled from exposure to an intense heat, burned imageless. Zee entered, and the tiles crushed to ash beneath his sneakers. He stood numb in the scorched and shrunken room. The seat of the fire-glossed toilet had curled to the shape of a black butterfly, and the sink counter that had held toothbrush and shaving implements was reduced to twisted clinkers.

The police, later, would classify the fire as un-classifiable. No human remains were found, and Carl was recorded as a missing person.

Caitlin and Sheelagh came by late in the afternoon

to see the mess for themselves, and they found Zee still there.

"What do you think happened?" Caitlin asked after she had surveyed the blasted room.

Zee was sitting on the couch in the living area where he could see into the bathroom, staring as though he had not heard her. He tugged at his beard, twisting at the braid that had formed from his daylong tugging. "Spontaneous human combustion," he whispered without looking at her.

"What?" The old woman looked to her daughter, who just shook her tear-streaked face.

"No one knows why," Zee answered in a trance, "but it happens all the time—usually to old ladies who drink too much."

Caitlin gave him a fierce, reproving look.

"I'm not joking," he shot back. "That's the statistic. Men burn up, too. And I guess that's what's happened to Carl."

"You mean, he just caught fire?" Caitlin sat down beside him and peered into his face incredulously. "How can that be?"

"I don't know. Nobody knows. I read about it once. The best theory they have is that imbibed alcohol ignites some kind of chemical reaction in the body."

"But Carl never drinks," Sheelagh pointed out, and then straightened with the rise of a memory. "The police came by the tavern. I told them he was feeling odd yesterday. Paper stuck to him and sparks kept jumping from his fingers."

"Yeah, I remember that," Zee muttered. He stood up. He went back to the bathroom for another look at the mystery. He was a rational man, and he felt, muscularly felt, that there was a reason for this.

The blue, wide-sky fragrance was almost gone. Sunlight slanted through the apartment window and laid a diagonal bar across the purpled bathroom mirror. In the brilliant yellow shaft, a shadow showed within the heat-varnish of the mirror.

"Hey!" he called to the two women. "Do you see this? Or am I losing my mind?"

Caitlin and Sheelagh entered the bathroom with trepid alertness and peered where Zee was pointing. In the violet-black sheen of the mirror, where the sunlight crawled, was the vaguest shadow.

"It looks like a tree crown to me," Caitlin said.

"No—it's the outline of a head, neck, and shoulders," Zee insisted, his finger frantically outlining the image.

"Could be," Sheelagh conceded. "But it could also just be our imagination."

"I'm a science writer," Zee said impatiently, pressing his face to the mirror. "I don't have an imagination. Get me a screwdriver. Come on."

Zee dismantled the mirror and took it to his studio office in Union Square. For a while he experimented with it himself, illuminating the surface with sunlight, arc light, UV light. Nothing more than the dimmest semblance of a human head appeared. And the rorschached shape could really have been anything. But Zee recognized the square of Carl's head, the familiar silhouette so oft-seen in the darkness of lights-out at St. Tim's, too well remembered from those lonely first years when a friend was the closest he got to family. Hard as he tried, though, his amplifications distinguished little more than an amorphous shadow.

Then a friend of his who worked at IBM's image-intensification lab in Jersey took pity on his feeble but relentless efforts and decided to prove once and for all that the mirror was a random fire pattern. A week later, the friend, pastier and meeker-looking, presented him with a computer-enhanced photograph. The five-by-seven-inch unglossed image showed a starburst of puissant radiance, most of it blank with an unscaled intensity. Daggered at the very center, a clot of darkness resolved with a stabbing clarity to Carl Schirmer's horror-crazed features.

Eating the Strange

Nothing—the blankest word in the language. A year ago, Carl Schirmer vanished into nothing. How? I've come to believe that the microevents in the atoms of Carl's body are the key. I'm not a physicist, but I know enough science to guess what happened to him. Here's what I figure:

The very big and the very small—general relativity and quantum mechanics—come together at a fundamental unit of length called Planck's length, which is the geometrical mean of Compton's wavelength and Einstein's gravitational radius of a particle. It looks like this:

$$1 = \sqrt{\frac{hf}{C^3}}$$

It's equivalent to about 10^{-33} centimeter. The edge of nothingness. Just beyond that smallness, spacetime itself loses the flat, continuous shape we take for granted and becomes a fantastic seething of wormholes and microbridges, the tiniest webs and bubblings. Any part of this ceaseless ferment lasts no more than the sheerest fraction of a second. It is the texture of Nothing. Like sponge. Or suds. Each bubble is a solitary region of space: The surface of the bubble is the farthest distance the center of the bubble can know about in its brief lifespan because that's as far as light can travel in so short a time. It's a universe in itself, existing only for that fraction of time and during that fraction connecting our universe with the ubiquitous Field that connects all universes.

To see how this fact connects with Carl Schirmer, we have to go back to Planck. At the end of the nineteenth century, he was trying to explain why radiation varies with temperature. As an object is heated, first it gets red-hot, then white-hot. It only gets blue-hot if the temperature increases. The higher frequencies of blue require more energy—which was news in the nineteenth century. Greater energy for *shorter* wavelengths! Not what common sense had learned from sound and water waves, which need more energy the *longer* they are. The now classic formula that predicts this phenomenon is $E = hF$, where $h = $ Planck's constant.

Since frequency is the inverse of time, the formula can be written this way: $E \times T = $ Constant (h). Energy, as everybody knows, equals mc^2, mass times the speed of light squared. What, after all, is the speed of light but a length of space covered in a period of time. So, h actually equals Mass times Length^2/Time. ML^2/T is called angular momentum.

What is it? Basically, it's linear momentum times the radius around which it spins, $ML/T \times L = ML^2/T$, like a rock in a sling. The amazing thing is that this angular momentum, alias Planck's constant, can hold any amount of energy at all! Like the skater who spins faster by pulling in his arms, the frequency of a photon increases as its radius, in this case wavelength, decreases. Fantastically, there is no limit to this increase of energy, either. The smaller the photon, the more energy it contains!

Somehow, Carl turned into light. And that light did not wholly irradiate away. If it had, a large part of Manhattan would have been vaporized. Instead, the photons that made up Carl increased in energy and *shrank*. The energy flux was so great that Carl's body of light shrank smaller than the fine structure of spacetime itself—and he fell through the fabric of our reality into the seething superspace of quantal-tunnels, spume, and foam—perhaps to expand again in another universe. This is the ghost hole theory. A saner phrase than Nothing. But really, it's just as senseless.

I'm writing a science fiction novel. *Shards of Time*. It's about Carl, of course, and the ghost hole that swallowed him. Just now it's seeming that's all there is between me and insanity—this fabulous story of a man who turns into light, a man whose fate I'd always taken for granted. Why are stories so long? The text is already there, in the true history of accidents that brought Carl and me together and then separated us. If I can just write it before my funds dry up, I may be able to sell it and not have to move. I don't want to move. There's been enough erasure lately. I've barely the stamina left to imagine the lies that can carry the ideas coming at me. The moment goes everywhere at once. Unfortunately, the muscle of my memory is numb, and my line of concentration has been wavering. I must rest. Actually, I must restructure myself inside out. Perhaps I'll fast.

That's one way to restructure and save money at the same time.

Caitlin Sweeney came to see me. The old lady was surprised at this mess. She didn't know I'd lost my teaching post. I think she was drunk. She wanted to see the mirror and the photo again, and she sat for a long time by the window looking at them. She wanted to know what they meant. I was five or six gins into forgetting that day, and I told her everything I've guessed about the ghost hole. When I was done, she asked why other scientists weren't studying what had happened to Carl. I tried to tell her that the mirror had become scientifically inadmissible after I took it off the wall, but I cracked up—laughing as much as crying—and that scared her off. Later, as it was growing darker and I was coming up from that day's drunk, I remembered her bird-bright eyes and the queer way she peered at the photo close up, the silver of her breath cutting the gloss again and again until she was sure of what she was seeing. And now *I'm* sure. Carl isn't screaming with pain in this photo. He's grimacing with intense pleasure!

—excerpts from *The Decomposition Notebook* by Zeke Zhdarnov

Orgasm ignited him. Hot as the sun's weight, space molded his shape. He tried to move but could not budge the pleasure. He tried to see and saw a hard blue sky, deeper than his sight, quivering with delight. Listening, he heard his heart moaning and his blood sizzling in his ears.

The voltage of the orgasm wearied, and the him-shaped heat melted to a delicate warmth.

"YOU ARE AWAKE!" A blowtorch voice seared his hearing, and his whole being juddered.

"Excuse me," the voice said more softly, deep as a man's but lissome as a woman's. The words came from every direction. "Can you tell me who you are?"

He tried to speak, but his voice had to cross a dreamgap between his will and his breath. When at last the words came, the sound of his voice subtracted him from the pleasurable stillness, and he immediately felt himself upfalling, floating and turning through the blue nothing: "Who wants to know?"

Carl drifted a long time. Blue filled the hollow bodiless center of his mind with peace. Memory was a soft distance. Expectation was unbegun.

So when the voice returned, directionless as smoke, intimate as a friend, the words embraced all of him, and he listened rapt as the face of the world—

"At the end of time, in the last million years of the universe, an unusual creature drifts through the slow hurry of evolution into the glory and anguish of self-awareness. It is an eld skyle, and it is I. I am vast by human standards: a cubic kilometer of silaceous cell matrices intricately and delicately interpenetrating. A colossal jellyfish floating in a lake: a radiolarial system, highly evolved, yet stationary and witless-looking as a brain without a body. To you I would look like a cloudy pond shimmering with biotic iridescence. Yet what makes me unusual is not my size or unlikely form. I am unusual because I thrive almost wholly on ghosts. I eat the past."

"Wait a minute! Hold on now!" Carl called through the thickness of the nightmare. "Are you saying I'm alive? This isn't the next world?"

"It's *another* world, Carl," the gray voice answered.

"How do you know my name?"

"I know everything about you."

"Are you—God?"

A hearty laugh towered like a megalith. "No. I'm as mortal as you. That's why I can assure you—you're not dead."

"How come I feel I should be?"

"Perhaps because you are, at this moment, bodiless."

"And you call that alive?" The propinquity of madness alarmed him. "Where am I? I can't see myself."

"You are inside me. I am reshaping you. To even begin to understand how this is possible, you must know something about my world. I live in a special region *inside* the cosmic black hole at the end of time. The universe around me is small and hot. Spacetime has long ago completed its expansion, braked, and begun to fall back on itself. At the time of this telling, one hundred and twenty-five billion years after your star, Sol, cindered to frozen rubble, the whole universe is a mere six hundred thousand parsecs wide, the distance from your earth to the Andromeda galaxy. All of spacetime has been reduced to a mote of what you knew the cosmos to be."

"I knew the cosmos to go from Brooklyn to the Bronx," Carl's voice quaked. "Where am I?"

"I've told you. You're at the end of time."

"But why?" Carl whined. "I was just at home, taking a shower—"

"One hundred and thirty billion years ago."

"I'm hallucinating. I must be hallucinating."

"Would you rather not hear this?"

"I have a choice?"

"Of course." The eld skyle's voice had the long patience of a horizon. "I am narrowing my five-space consciousness to your human smallness because it pleasures me. It's not at all necessary. If you prefer, I'll just pass you on into my world. Words are useful only if you can believe them. In your case, perhaps, experience itself is the best teacher."

"Well, if you put it that way—go ahead, tell me everything."

The blue space holding Carl brightened like the fever of a dream. "I'm glad, Carl. I've wanted to tell this story for a long time. Let me begin again. We are now in a place many years in your future. So far in the future that the universe itself is old and dying. It is caving in on itself. In the whirlpool center of this implosion, the most immense collapsar that has ever existed spins, tusked with fiery streamers huge as galaxies. The void around it flares with its radiant scud, too hot for planets or even ordinary stars. But inside the black hole, beyond its cyclone of neutron fire, where all things, even the subtleties of light, are spellbound by gravity, a wonderful kingdom exists."

"And that's where we are now, right?"

"Yes. The kingdom is called the World. It is a lightsecond deep, and it is wide as thirteen earths. Most remarkable of all, it is embedded in a bubble of ordinary spacetime, a gravitational globule suspended inside the black hole. The spin of the collapsar's ring nucleus distorts the infalling spacetime around the vacuole kingdom, sealing the World off from the crushing gravity that surrounds it on all sides. The nucleus of the black hole is the kingdom's source of life, much the way Sol was the lifesource of your planet—only in reverse. Sol was a star, and it radiated the energy which sustained earthlife. The ring nucleus here is a singularity, an infinitely dense zone where light and spacetime cease to exist. The singularity pulls energy into it. The radiation streaming past and through the World provides the light and energy for life to thrive. After passing here, the energy plunges on, into the nucleus, where it is destroyed. Except at the exact center. There a hole in the ring singularity links into superspace, an infinite corridor that connects all the universes that exist—the multiverse. You popped out of that hole."

"Any chance I could pop back in?" Carl queried hopefully.

"I'm afraid not. You see, you came out as light. And most of you was lost in the ring singularity. Only some of you shot straight through the hole of the ring, arced along a klein-bottle warp, looking from the center of the black hole to the periphery before plummeting back toward the core. Along the way, your four-space journey intersected the top edge of this kingdom and glinted here in this living lake—in me. A few of your photons were captured by specialized cells just under the glassy surface of my lake, and over a period of time equal to an earth century, you were re-created from the information inside your own light."

Carl felt frosty with fear. "How do you know you got it right?"

"Every molecule of your form has been explored by my five-space consciousness and compared to the anthropic ideal enfolded in the hyperspace of your genes. The flaws and variances of the genetic ideal were the rough edges of your individuality: your soft stomach, weak eyes, bald head, and bloated kidneys. Those deviations from the perfection implicit in your chromosomes are actually food to a being like me—an eld skyle. I eat the strange. You see, my five-space mind experiences you wholly, shining with the full possibilities of life. There is a great potential difference between that and your actual physical form. An eld skyle experiences a thrilling, century-long rush of power as it rectifies the dimensionally charged gap between the optimal and the actual."

"Yeah, well, I'm glad this was a high for somebody. But what's it do for me?"

"What I've done for you, Carl"—the eld skyle

spoke with the exuberance of a game-show host—"is to give you a new body. It's fashioned from the lake sludge, but it's more fully you than the old shape you endured. Your body has been adamized, if you will accept my neologism. Like Adam, you have now been made in the exact likeness of your nucleic potential. You have been both exalted and reduced. Your individuality is potentially less but your actual expression, your stock strength, your innate animality, is greater."

"Sounds great as an idea," Carl admitted, "but is it me?"

"Apart from your new appearance," the eld skyle's voice hushed through him, "you won't feel any differently than you did one hundred and thirty billion years ago on earth. You are still essentially yourself. Even your memories are intact. Let me show you—"

The presence of the eld skyle's voice vanished into a bleat of silence. Anxiety shivered through Carl as the conviction that he was not dreaming seized him. And then the glistening pleasure returned. His fear shriveled. He had no idea what was happening, but felt no fear at all. Warmingly, the blue void that surrounded and buoyed him shimmered with movement. The light jellied to images, glassy shapes from his past: St. Tim's ash-colored buildings, canyoned Manhattan, the Blue Apple's dirty bricks glowing in the city's crooked daylight. Faces snapped past like the rags of fireworks: childhood buddies, teachers, lovers, bosses, and his closest friend, Zeke, ZeeZee, Zeebo, the Zee, his first hero, the big kid who had protected him from the bullies, the grown man Carl had helped grapple with his feelings after Nam and a divorce—

Gone.

Dumbstruck and glowing with new feelings, Carl rolled gently through the blue emptiness.

"As you see, your history is still with you," the

voice returned, slender. "So is your fear. But I'm holding it in check because you are from a special era of life. You have the possibility of apprehending your fate, unlike the thousands of other humans from earlier times that have given their strangeness to me and gone on. They had no way of grasping the concept of a final black hole or this marvelous kingdom dangling within it. You are the first that I can speak to about the infinity virus."

"I think you're overrating me."

"No. I am using concepts your brain has already encountered."

"Right, but my brain's a lot smarter than I am. Just take it slow."

"Certainly," the eld skyle agreed, sounding very close in the whaled space. "The infinity virus arrived a billion years ago. It came through the ring hole from somewhere in the multiverse. It carried the information to build me and all the other lifeforms in the World. There is no archaeological evidence of life older than a billion years ago anywhere in the kingdom. None of the many intelligences that live here now know where the virus came from. Also, none of the lifeforms that evolved from the infinity virus are humanoid. All the people in the Werld have come here through eld skyles, as you've come here."

"You mean—I'm not alone? There are other *humans* here?"

"Oh, yes. All of them, or their ancestors, have come through me and my kind. We are the most evolved product of the viral program. Our five-space awareness is sustained by three primary factors: light infalling through the collapsar's event horizon, the mineral honeycomb of the rock that holds our liquid forms, and the dimensional charge from assimilating the strangeness of other creatures. To satisfy the last of these needs, eld skyles are equipped with a unique spore designed very much like its viral ancestor. The spore is encoded to activate only inside neurologies broadcasting a certain frequency indicative of self-awareness. After it is formed and programmed, it is iridium-coated and ejected through a waterspout high into the atmosphere. There its glide-shape catches the powerful axial winds of the Werld, and it is propelled into the fibrous, filament-wide tunnels that connect the fringes of the gravity bubble with the superspace in the open center of the singularity."

"All this for a meal?" Carl was giddy with the weirdness of his predicament. "You're a five-space being and you haven't even invented fast food yet? Come on."

"This does sound complex from a three-space view, I grant you. But let me go on. It takes my spore years to reach the hole in the singularity, but the instant it gets there, it vanishes into the multiverse and just as instantly appears somewhere in the infinite elsewhere. Of course, most of the spores are lost. Even with their iridium armor, the heat of the stars and the far greater endlessness of space defeat them. Only the tiniest fraction of the trillions of spores ejected by an eld skyle ever find their way to a useful environment."

"Well, you're obviously doing something right."

"Yes, indeed. Entirely by chance, one spore reached the planet earth eighty-four million years before you were born. It hovered in the reservoir of ionic detritus of the upper atmosphere for a hundred thousand years or so before sifting down into the biosphere. A fish ate it first, and the molecular lock of the spore's surface bonded it to the nerve tissue of the creature. The spore passed along from animal to animal as food for millions of years. For a long while it lapsed into the limbo of silt before being taken up by a plant, eaten, and carried once again by the life frenzy. Thirty-two thousand years ago, the spore was eaten in a piece of badger meat by a lake-dweller in neolithic Switzerland. That was one of your ancestors."

"No wonder I'm a vegetarian."

"The frequency of her neurology was complex enough to activate the spore, which immediately sited itself in her genetic material. Fifteen hundred generations later, the spore received a subquantal signal from me, the eld skyle that began its journey one hundred and thirty billion years in the future. That signal is the key to this whole cycle. It is an inertial wave signal and propagates through superspace instantly. My need is felt everywhere that my spores are, for the spores are inertially identical to me. My five-space mind selects an activated spore from somewhere in creation by sensing and evaluating the complexity of the spores' hosts, and at my discretion, the chosen spore begins its delivery."

"So—bingo—here I am."

"Would you like to hear more about the mechanism of your journey?"

"Why not?"

"As soon as I selected you, the spore's master program went to work on two fronts—your body's neuromolecular field and your universe's inertial field."

"You've already lost me."

"Bear with me. The spore flooded your body with a complexly designed substance modeled on your body's natural neurotransmitters. It mimed your own nerve chemicals so that it could penetrate the RNA in the synapses of your nerves. Within forty-eight hours, every RNA molecule in your body's synapses was fitted with the spore's neurochemical. The spore chemical modulated your nerve impulses, triggering a neural feedback pattern in your sensory ganglia, brain stem, and limbic area that you experienced as intense, inexplicable euphoria. But that was a mere side effect."

"I'm beginning to feel that *I'm* just a side effect," Carl despaired.

"In a manner of speaking, you are. You're a projection of your body. The main thrust of the spore saturation was to generate a waveform hologram of your body, inside out, atom by atom. Once that waveform came on, the electric resonance of your nervous system began harmonizing with the magnetic field of the earth. The harmonic buzz charged you with the billion-volt potential difference between the ionosphere and the earth. You were walking lightning."

"That explains why I was sparking all day."

"Yes, that took the better part of a day. But what happened next happened swiftly. The wave resonance of you and the planet began to pick up the overtonal harmonics of the sun's field, the local stars, even the galaxy. By that time, you were hypercharged, and the water in your shower was sustaining such strong transfer charge that it was flying away from your body. Your waveform was in resonance with the charge of the universe itself. A few moments later you reached concrescence, the point where the resonation of you and the universe was precise enough to supply the energy for a local collapse. In a sliver of a second, the immense energy transfer from the universe shrank your light pattern into a space smaller than ten to the minus forty-third centimeter, smaller than the grain of space-time. Your collapsed waveform fell into a hypertubule, a wormhole entrance into the multiverse smaller than a quark. The inertial imprint of the spore guided you here. And so the circle joins."

The voice vanished again, and Carl's body tightened with the silence. Ahead of him, space wrinkled, and a warp of sunlight spalled the blue distance.

"You're surfacing now," the eld skyle spoke. "You're

rising out of my watery depths. You've listened patiently, and finally it's time for you to confront your new life."

"Hey, not yet," Carl called out. "You haven't told me anything about this place."

Tremulous, sudden brilliance stunned Carl. He felt the rising rush of his body. His back arched, and just as he realized that he *was* indeed in water, he split the surface like a man collapsing. The air gulped him, and his hungry lungs ached with the cold. As he splashed to his back, lurching and flapping to find his balance, his senses swooped in on him.

Haws of birdnoise burst on all sides, and a flock of snakeheaded blue egrets swarmed off the water and into the air. The sky was a radiant purple, sunless yet gleaming. Its brightness heaved off the water and hurt his eyes.

"Jesus Flippin' Christ," he gasped, the words cold in his mouth.

The snaky egrets were flapping toward a boulder-stubbled shore. He swam after them even though he did not know how to swim. The water he was in was thicker than water, so buoyant it was holding him up. His meagerest efforts to move were enough to spin him wildly, and several moments passed before he coordinated himself to move in one direction. By then, his eyes had adjusted to the slam of the strong light, and he could see the shore more clearly. It wasn't a shore. It was a rim—a wall. The boulders were immense. The bigger ones on either side of him were small islands wraithed with misty flowers. Ahead, the blue egrets landed on their reflections in the bright shallows.

"Before you reach my edge, I do have something more to tell you." The sound of the voice was alarming. It seemed to come from all around. Carl whirled. After he had calmed himself and begun sliding toward the shallows again, the eld skyle's lucent voice continued:

"The Werld is vast, Carl. Its appearance will awe you, for you've never seen anything like it. Crags of tree-crowded rock floating in space, glinting with waterfalls and rainbows, the purple sky around them swarming with their shadows and the tumbling clouds. It's beautiful beyond words. Hard, even for me, to believe that when the infinity virus first arrived here, there was nothing but infalling cosmic dust and light. The virus proliferated close to the inside of the event horizon in the high-energy light and collected the cosmic dust into exoskeletons. That served as shields, allowing the organism to draw even closer to its power source. Like coral, only much faster, the exoskeletons accumulated along the fields of force laced throughout this gravity vacuole. Over millions of years, planetoids formed around the standing resonance patterns of those gravity waves. The gaseous emissions of the swiftly evolving viral descendants created a watery, oxygen-bright atmosphere which now is only slightly richer than the one you once breathed."

The sky was so bright that Carl had to float face-down. When he turned his head for air, he asked: where are the people you said were around?"

"Many sentient lifeforms are present in the Werld at this time," the eld skyle answered, its voice sounding as if it spoke from the core of his brain. "Few are humanoid. In fact, the most technologically advanced planetoid, Galgul, is occupied by the predominate sentience of the Werld—the zōtl. They're arachnoid creatures that exist as fused male-female units. The female is almost twice the size of a human and apparently featureless—a black, furry barrel to your eyes—but quite intelligent. The males are smaller, not as bright, but very deft and fast. They're spidery, about the size of your hand, and red or black depending on their social status. They've adapted four of their eight appendages into wings, and they can hover or soar. Their other four legs are actually arms with powerful and agile grippers. They see with remarkable acuity in infrared and your visible range. Most of their communications are hormonal, though they also have a click language several orders more complex than dolphin speech. The male-female components must unite regularly to survive, since each half alone completes only part of their metabolic cycle. They eat nitrogen, light, and the pain-products of other creatures. Here in the World, their favorite food is humans."

"Great. You've eaten my strange, and they want to eat the rest."

"I'm warning you about the zōtl because once you go over my edge, you'll be beyond my reach. The zōtl are as intelligent as humans, with a technology of their own. They herd humans and use them as they need. A zōtl feast is ghastly. The male zōtl piths the back of the skull, and a needle-fine tubule is inserted into the amygdala, the pain center of the brain. The human is paralyzed but quite aware of what is happening. The awareness is important to the zōtl's digestion, so the captive brain is injected with a serum that heightens perceptions. Then the pain center is activated, and the human suffers. The torment is horrendous, a molten tearing, all the more terrible because the body is left intact and is nourished by the zōtl's glucose wastes. The feeding can last for weeks."

"I want to go home!" Carl cried and rolled to his back in the thick water. His white body gleamed in the hot light. "Look at me—I'm naked. How can I defend myself naked?"

"The only defense against the zōtl for you is to avoid them. There is a tribe of humans at your level of development who live avoidance. They have no advanced technology, as that would attract zōtl hunt-

33

ers; however, their culture is rich. I've inscribed their language in your brain, and you'll have no trouble communicating with them. They call themselves Foke. I've arranged for a thornwing, a kind of bird-plant, to take you to Tarfeather, the Foke's present secret home. And to complete my birthing of you as a man, I've modified your sex hormone, alpha androstenol, to attract a woman I know of among the Foke. Her name is Evoë, and she knows the World. If you treat her wisely, she will be your best ally."

Carl's backstroke picked up as a gigantic sense of future rose in him. "I don't know what to say."

"Then listen. There are a few more things you should know about the World. The scattered foci of gravity nodes that give the Werld its unique contours also magnetize space in such a way that the unwinding of your supercoiled DNA is inhibited. Which means you won't age. Genetic chipping by cosmic rays is limited at the Midwerld level of the Foke by the atmosphere and the planetoids between them and the horizon, where the radiation enters. And there are as yet no viral cancers, colds, or diseases. Death is an accident here. And there is bounteous opportunity for accidents, for the gravity contours and the winds of the Werld are treacherous. Not to mention gumper hogs with maws like sharks, poison dagger lizards, and man-sized blood beetles. Learn well what the Foke have to teach you, and you will live long."

"Oh, God, eld skyle," Carl moaned. "I feel like fishfood floating in an aquarium. Can't you give me a gun or a knife or even some clothes?"

The eld skyle's voice was gone. Only the water-lammed sounds of the shore filled his hearing.

Carl's efforts had carried him over the slippery surface to the shore. Black sand dimpled under his hands as he pushed himself to his knees. The shallow water unruffled, and he saw a red-bearded, brass-haired man with a square-boned face and thick shoulders. It was he. Those tentative hazel eyes were his own. He reached out and touched the blindness of the water. The reflection wobbled. Slow with disbelief, he lifted his arms and stared at the circuitry of veins and the straps of muscle straining for use. His chest was smoky with russet hair and his abdomen squared with strength. The blood-drum beat louder as his wavering fingertips followed the taut planes of his face to his mane of sleek, redgold hair. Suddenly, the silence of the eld skyle was more real than its voice had been, and Carl sat back in the thick water as what it had said recurred to him.

"Adamized," he mouthed, peering at his reflection, tugging at his hair, and grinning like a lunatic. The numbness of the eld skyle's ecstasy was thinning, tingling with the implications of all Carl had just learned.

"Carl Schirmer," he said to himself, "look what's happened to you. It can't be real. It is real, bumblewit. But it can't be. Eld skyle, if you can hear me—you did a great job. If only I could take this home with me."

He looked about to see where he was. The sandbar where he was kneeling curved into a black sand beach beneath eel-black dolmen rocks. Carl took one more look into the surprised explosions of his eyes, then heaved himself to his feet and slogged up the beach. The windhoned rocks were pitted and fractured, and even though he was naked, he had no difficulty scaling the rockface to the top.

A wall of wind surfed along the ledge, and he squinted against the cold rush and the brash sunlight at islands floating in the sky. For as far as he could see, huge chunks of rock floated in space, their irregular surfaces covered with slim, elegant trees and golden grass. The nearest skyle hovered several hundred meters away. Dark-green curtains of spruce draped cliffwalls

35

that banked a long lake. Another eld skyle, Carl realized, and he glanced back toward where he had come from. The glare off the water sprained his seeing, and he had to stare at the tree-staggered coast to clear his eyes. Trembling smells of cedar and pine riffled in the air, and hot light sighed off dusty rocks.

When he could see clearly again, he gazed back over the edge into the gulf of floating islands. Delirious cloudshapes obscured the distances, melted-looking sprawls of silver and gold archipelagoed with skyles. With astonishment he noticed that a waterfall at the bottom of a nearby skyle was falling upward, toward the skyle.

While he studied the apparent anomaly, a thick bark-tattered vine skirled its way along a fissure in the outside wall, moving serpentwise toward him. He was mentally reviewing what the eld skyle had told him about focalized gravity nodes when the slither vine curled over the edge and snagged his ankle.

"Ee-yow!" He jumped with fear and tripped forward, falling to his face. Another startled bark escaped him before the vine yanked him off the wall and into the abyss. The wind kicked the breath out of him, and he sprawled, expecting to fall. Instead, he flew sideways along the rimwall and plunged into a net of thorny meshed vines. The net snapped about him, enwrapping him tightly in a pod that broke away and plummeted into the gulf.

Carl's face was clear of the binding tendrils, and he could see the raptor of the pod's tiny hooked head and the taloned vines dangling below. The underside of the eld skyle swung into view, revealing another lake ringed with twisted trees, its surface velvety black.

Carl heard the flap of wings above him, and the thornwing caught a powerful current and swooped through a swarm of skyles. The tug of the abrupt curves squeezed his insides, and the physical reality of what was happening loomed up in him. As the thornwing glided through the bright tatters of cloud among the sky-hung buttes, he flashed to his old life—the Blue Apple, Caitlin, and Sheelagh. An astonished hilarity quaked in him, rippled with fear. The memory of the eld skyle's voice was all that reigned in his madness. One hundred and thirty *billion* years had passed. The wind of the thornwing's flight streamed over him, yet he was basted with sweat.

As they dropped deeper into the World, the light of the sky changed. Vast wells of peacock-blue space churned with golden clouds. Flocks of winged animals arrowed along flyways in all directions. And everywhere, kingdoms of black rock and blue forests hung in the air. Some of the skyles were so huge that skimming over them was like flying on earth again, watching the woods of Pennsylvania rolling by, until the edge curved past and the sky billowed with distance.

Among far-off skyles, glass towers flashed. Carl glimpsed them briefly before a metallic scream ripped his hearing to deafness. A finned black metal boomerang big as a Ferris wheel spun out from a tower of clouds and sliced through the air only meters away. The thornwing squawked and looped a tight arc, volplaning with the slipstream of the craft. Then the thornwing's glide cut through the interior of a cloud, and the oystery blankness obscured sight for a long time. The flightscream of the craft thinned with distance, and the thornwing rolled into a relaxed glide.

The diffuse light rusted as they went deeper. When they swooped out of the clouds, the World was dusky. Scarlet walls of cumulus toppled on all sides, and the hollows of the skyles brimmed with night.

Tiny lights winked from the darkside of a skyle. As the thornwing rushed closer, Carl saw that the sparks were lanterns held by shadowy figures. The thornwing arrowed toward the figures, the frayed tips of trees brushing past and the rocky forest floor hurtling by. They were dressed in animal skins and leather thongs. When they sighted the diving thornwing with its torpedoed passenger, their startled cries cracked the nocturnal silence, and they bolted.

They howled as they ran, conferring frenziedly while dodging branches and fallen trees. All at once, they halted and heaved their lanterns at the thornwing, The lanterns collided in midair and burst into a gush of sparks. Hot flechettes stung Carl along the length of his body, and he heard the thornwing's shrill cry as the burning embers caught in it shaggy hide.

Its tendriled embrace broke, and Carl collapsed onto the duff-cushioned ground. Flopped out on his back, he witnessed the thornwing's retreat. With its sheer wings withdrawn, it was a tangle of spiked vines and vetch. It rolled along the ground like a tumbleweed, glinting with the sparks it had caught, and finally unwrapping into a gawky, spiderlegged flap of bluegreen wings.

One of the fur-wrapped people snapped open a bow and swiftly strung an arrow. But as he was sighting the thornwing, Carl lurched at him and spoiled his shot. The thornwing arched overhead in time to see Carl thrown back to the ground. It rauked once and soared out of sight.

Hoots and shouts clattered in the chill air, and the fur-strapped people were around him. They chided his nakedness, his clumsiness, and his interference. And he understood them. Their language was a rushed sibilance, a strange whisper-tongue, yet he recognized it: "He let the flopwing get away! Break his wrist."

"Leave him be. He's nothing. Did you see him hit the ground like a bag of roots? Haw!"

"At least we can see he's a man," a woman's voice

added, "and a large-sized one at that!" Giggles and female voices fluttered.

"He's obviously an eld dropping," a male's coarse voice said. "Let's leave him here."

A shouted "No!" jumped from the women in the small crowd. "We must bring him to the wizan," one of the women spoke. "It is the law."

"Crawl!" The man's voice coarsed again. He stepped forward where Carl could see him: a bleak man in wolf and snakeskins, his youthful blackbearded face already sharp and hard as a flintedge. At his hip, in a lizardhide holster, was a handgun. "I'm the chief of this run, and I say we leave him. If he's alive when we circle back this way, we'll take him to Tarfeather."

"Right, Allin!" another of the men called out. "Let's get to Rhene and free our Foke now."

"Please, go," Carl agreed from where he was back-sprawled. He cast a glance over the forest-hackled ridges of the skyle. "I can make myself comfortable here if you'd leave me some clothes."

Silence boomed. Allin took one step closer to Carl. "You speak Foke."

"He's not a skyle dropping," one of the others guessed.

"I think I am," Carl said, sitting up. "The eld skyle gave me your language before sending me out into the Werld. You're the Foke, right? From Tarfeather."

Mutters shivered through the group. Allin hushed them with a slant of his cubed head. His black hair was pleated tightly to his skull and dangled in corded bangles to his shoulders. The small hairs at the crown of his forehead twitched. "You are the first dropping that I've heard speak." His tiny eyes were brown and flecked with gray glints as though they were sweating. "Where are you from?"

"Uh—earth. A planet that existed a very long time ago—"

Allin cut him off: "No, fool. Where in the Werld are you from?"

"The eld skyle?" Carl offered.

Allin snorted with frustration. One of the others stepped closer, a broadfaced woman with short, brindled hair; she said to Carl: "Allin wants to know where the thornwing picked you up. There are millions of eld skyles. What you saw on the path you flew from there to here could help us a great deal."

"Craw, it could save our lives!" Allin snapped.

"Did the thornwing fly the Cloudgate?" the brindle-haired woman asked. "You know the Cloudgate."

Of course he did. The information was there with the language, rising to his awareness as an image: Clouds swirled like the wheel of the galaxy, helixing a spiral that corkscrewed the length of the Werld. Because of the large-scale gravitational refraction of the infalling light, one side of the Werld glowed bluish and the other side ruddy. The direction of the cloud's drift toward either of those different sky colors told which side of the Werld one was on. Also, the intensity of the light revealed depth from the Eld, which was the fire of photons and nucleons falling through the event horizon. The Eld's antipode was the Rim, the land of night and the lower edge of the Werld where spacetime funneled rapidly toward the core of the black hole.

This information bristled in him, but he lacked the specific knowledge—he did not remember the shade of haze in the sky or the drift of the clouds. He told them as much, and Allin turned away from him with disgust.

"Wrap him up," the leader ordered, "and let's go. It's a long journey to Tarfeather."

Before Carl could react, several of the men seized him and bound him with leather cord in a plump,

40

scratchy blanket. Two men carried him like a rolled-up rug, and everyone ran through the trees toward the falloff of the ledge. Carl's head was free, and he saw the front runners bound off the cliff, somersault in midair, and shoot high into the sky.

Carl gawked to see the feet of the men carrying him rush through a crinkling of dead leaves to the edge of the ridge and leap. A veil of forest unfolded below them, and Carl clenched against the tug of gravity. Instead, the forest spread below him and retreated. A powerful undertow was hoisting them upward. The skyle they had been on fell away, and they were sailing swiftly into a lake of empty space. There, the contour of banked space leveled, and they positioned their bodies to glide in the direction of their choice.

Allin led them toward a keyhole of brilliant light among a cluster of skyles. The flight was a lengthy one, for on the other side of the cluster was another, huger sea of emptiness. Deprived of the familiar temporal rhythms of night and day, the many hours seemed interminable to Carl. For a while, he occupied himself with the wonder of his new experience. But that was too bulky. Everything was so new to him that the information that the eld skyle had implanted in him packed his mind, and nothing was clear.

He concentrated and saw the World in his mental eye the way the Foke did: The fierce light of the collapsing universe came through the Eld and fell first into the Welkyn, the upper Werld; then through the gold spiraling clouds to the crepuscular Midwerld, where they were now; and finally down into Rataros in the darkness at the World's edge—the Rim. Flexing his neck, he could see the arc of the sky and just barely discern the pastel difference in shades between the red and blue extremes. He dozed and pondered and dozed again.

Carl was roused when the men guiding him along their fallpath took a firm grip and pulled him sharply to one side. His insides lurched, and he woke to find himself gently rolling in the sky toward a tiny crevassed skyle. "Where are we?" he asked in English and then again in Foke.

"Be quiet," one of the carriers admonished. "We're being stalked."

They rotated him so that he could see the black, boomerang-shaped craft that was hovering a thousand meters away. It looked like a splinter in the dusk.

"They haven't seen us yet. We're going to hide and wait until—"

A star glinted at the head of the viper-flat craft, and the air around them thumped with the pressure of a nearby explosion. By the time the boom erupted, they had rolled through the sky to the other side of the skyle.

Another blast scythed the top off the small skyle and fountained the surrounding space with gravel.

The Foke touched down on the tiny skyle and kicked off again immediately, bounding toward the next nearest skyle. Before they reached it, the small skyle they had thrust off wobbled under repeated fire. The din ruptured hearing, and with a deafening force, the skyle shattered.

The pulverized rock spun away from a writhing, electric-blue bolt of ionized air. A spearhead of crushed stone pierced the skull of the man carrying Carl. His partner clutched at Carl, and the two whirled with the humbling force of the devastation.

A dizzying plunge whipped seeing to a blur. Impact jolted sense out of Carl, and he lay spraddled face up, staring at the distant black grin of the killer ship.

"Get up, you fool!" Allin's angry voice cut deeper than Carl's daze.

Carl sat up and realized that the binding straps had burst. The rug moved slickly under him. He had landed on the man who was carrying him. The dead man's face was twisted around a purple scream.

"Come on, idiot!" Allin shouted again. "Get over here before they fire again."

Carl staggered to his feet and gawked at the spired precipice he was on. Allin was waving to him from another skyle across a gap that dropped into gaudy, cloud-fiery distances.

Carl balked. Allin called out once more: "Just leap as hard as you can! The fallpath will carry you."

Carl's muscles were stymied with fear. Allin moved to bound toward him, but at that moment the gunship fired again. A brain-stuffing roar shook Carl to his knees. The ship had hit the spired skyle he was on.

Voices cried through the muddy echoes of the blast. He looked up and saw five of the Foke vaulting toward him. The sight of them coming for him stood him up. He waved, the ship flashed again, and the five flyers burst like blood bags.

Allin roared and leaped into space. He shot over the gap and rammed headlong into Carl, hurtling them both off the spire as it splattered under a direct hit.

Carl retched for breath and glimpsed veins of inky dust bleeding into the alien sky—glimpsed streaming manes of blood and a blue tangle of intestine—before Allin hit him and soared him into darkness.

He came around a minute later, and they were lying in the tall grass on the edge of another skyle. The blow had unlocked his clarity, and he saw with sharp precision for the first time. His head was twanging with pain, his sight greasy with tears, and he quaked with the memory of his cowardice and the grim result. But for once, he recognized the truth of where he was. Overhead, the corpses were unwrapping in the flow of the fallpath. In a cloud of blood, ravelings of entrails wavered like a shredded banner, and heads and limbs in rags of flesh toppled in a slow spin.

Behind the spur of rock where they lay, the gunship waited. Its name shimmered into Carl's awareness: It was a zōtl jumpship—perhaps *the* zōtl jumpship that he had seen earlier when the thornwing was gliding with him through the Welkyn. Now that he remembered, he was convinced that the ship had been arcing down toward these gloaming levels. It would wait to see if there was movement. The zōtl's detectors were useless against them, because they had no radios and little metal with them, apart from Allin's pistol. The jumpship was a carrier vessel and would be reluctant to come closer. Too many others had been destroyed by plastique bombs. That understanding settled Carl into a wait, though his insides were jangling with what had just happened.

He pressed his back into the wet ground under him and stared through the mess of broken shapes at the motes of skyles hanging higher than his sight into the tottering reaches. And in that moment, under the fluttering smoke of smashed bodies, lives lost to save him, he awoke.

Until the keen agony of that time, he had merely been a name, Carl Schirmer, in an endless life that could have been happening on earth or in the World or anywhere. He was just the shadow of his smiles and words and habits. He was just the scree of time, a jumble of genetic and historical accidents that he called I. He had been too muddy with flaws and selfish emotions to carry any reflection, so he never really was self-aware, he never was an I, until he had been chased to the tip of death.

Lying there, watching the flame-antlered clouds and, nearer, the drifting gore of the dead, the voltage of his life sizzled into awareness. His hard brain went soft, and he felt his livingness as never before. His body was strong, powerful even, and the animal tension in his nerves smoldered in his muscles, eager for movement.

The eld skyle had indeed adamized Carl, for he had never experienced before the integrity of bone and tendon that he knew now. A new health, made terribly alert by contrast to the stew of body parts swimming above him, centered his perceptions. All at once, Carl was an I, an ephemeral summoning of minerals, water, and light into mind. The gruesome deaths of the five Foke jarred him into the itchy, gummy, renitent physicality of his body. The adamized changes made that immersion easier and more palatable. His flat feet were gone and the achy calves that went with them. The hair on his hulled chest had the glow of fur. And the vitality of his lifeforce stretched him above the dumbness of his meat into the unchangeable domain of I.

"Let's go," Allin breathed from nearby.

His voice sharpened Carl's focus, and Carl felt the chill air gnawing him. He was still naked. He rolled to his side and saw Allin bellycrawling deeper into the long grass. He scuttled after him, ignoring the switching cuts of the blades and the thistly ground. At the far end of the long field, the earth (*ah, ironic word*) crumbled into a deep deciduous pit.

"We're going to jump again," Allin told him. His red eyes were a smear of disdain. "Do you think you can do it?"

The side of Carl's jaw where Allin had hit him pulsed louder. "Hell, let's go."

Allin pushed to his feet, dashed to the lip of the pit, and leaped upward.

Carl followed. His urgency to embrace this miraculous life erased his fear, and he lunged off the precipice.

The upward undertow snagged him at once, and he lofted on the cold wind into the opal sky of Midwerld.

Allin had techniques for riding the fallpath that allowed him to vary his speed and direction. He bowed his body, reaching behind him for his ankles and the straps of his strider sandals. He slowed and slid back until he was beside Carl. He took some moments to show Carl how to hold himself—sleeking himself for speed and twisting for direction. The Foke used the flaps of furs like sails to steer himself. *Finsuit*, the term came to Carl.

Carl glanced back but did not see the black splinter of the jumpship. When he looked forward again, he noticed the survivors of the group circling ahead. They were furious at him, and he couldn't blame them. He had shown himself a coward, and if he'd had a tail, it would have been tucked.

They gave him clothes, a spare ill-fitting finsuit and tight strider sandals—but for the remainder of the flight, no one spoke to him. The journey lasted longer than he could guess. He was given a horn of water and purple twists of meat tough and spicy as jerky. As the sky indigoed and the great gorges of cloud glowered a longer red, he had plenty of time to ponder his situation.

He carefully reviewed everything he could remember of what the eld skyle had told him, and he explored further the remarkable information that imbued the Foke language he had been given. He contemplated Foke time. The gravitationally refracted colors that banded the whole Werld turned slowly, completing a full rotation in a span of time he estimated was equal to his sense of a century. The Foke who survived that long were called wizan. They were the tribe's spiritual leaders, contemplators of time, being, even question. He knew they would orient him, but he couldn't have guessed then how profoundly.

Tarfeather was the nomadic home of the Foke. Thousands of people lived there, migrating in continuous advance groups to test other regions of the World for the future locales of Tarfeather. The speed of the endless journey varied. When Carl arrived, the site was well settled. Skyles for many kilometers around showed signs of cultivation: grazing herds, farmland, tree homes, and the sky busy with the movement of people and barges. The fallpaths were distinct with activity, and he could clearly discern the network of gravity-curved flightlanes that enmeshed the skyles.

The band progressed toward the largest skyle, a mountain range extending both up and down and with an encircling river curling about the equator. The valleys were jungles, and all the prominences and abutments that jutted away from the skyle were naked rock.

Closer, Carl recognized black-and-gray camouflage tents. Bright-blue-robed figures were rushing out of one tent onto the fallpath to meet the returning group.

Allin had taken the lead when they entered Tarfeather, flashing mirror signals long before Carl saw any sign of a settlement. He saluted the squad when they approached and recounted how Carl had been discovered and seven of the group lost.

Carl studied their faces. They had the same racial characteristics as the people who had found him: dark and striated hair, broad bones, cinnamon-toned skin, and flecked, agate-banded eyes. They were used faces, and they did not return his stare kindly.

They said nothing directly to Carl until they helped him land—a trickier maneuver than taking off. He stumbled with the abruptness of the shift from glide to fall and had to be helped to his feet. It was like stepping out of a pool after a long swim. The gravity owned him, and he slumped along the rock path with the others to one of the larger tents.

The interior had the walnut smell of autumn and a soft sheen of woodsmoke. Sheets of light hung from slit windows in the tent roof. The long hall looked as busy as a bazaar, yet the sound level mimed a temple.

Carl was led swiftly as his ponderous legs could keep up through the silky warmth, past curtained stalls of conversing people—office, food stalls, gamerooms—till they came to a stall with only one man in it. He was dressed in black and stood out boldly against the intricate cloud tapestry behind him.

The others regarded him deferentially, and Allin greeted him as wizan. "He speaks the language, sir. Perfectly."

"Is that so?" The wizan appeared younger than any of them. His immaculately groomed features seemed mild as amber.

"Yes," Carl replied. "An eld skyle imprinted it in my brain. Then I was sent to the Foke in a thornwing. It's the craziest thing that's ever happened to me—"

"Yes," the wizan cut him off, "the eld skyles are sometimes helpful in those ways." He was seated on a cushion, still and square as a Mayan icon. "You don't look much like a Foke, but you are clearly human and strong-looking at that. From where did the eld skyle take you?"

"I'm from the planet called earth." The words felt like tinsel in his mouth. "It existed a long time ago."

"What position did you have in your world?"

Carl couldn't find the words *businessman* or *bartender* in the Foke language. "I was a trader and brewseller."

The wizan sighed softly with disappointment.

"He's just a dropping that knows how to talk," Allin said. "He's not useful. I sensed that when we found him, but the others insisted that he be brought here. On the way, seven of ours were killed. A zōtl jumpship. I've passed the location along and a strike force is on the way."

The wizan silenced him with a limp wave. "What is your name?" he asked Carl.

"Carl."

"Carl, do you want to stay with us?"

"The eld skyle sent me to you," Carl answered. "He warned me about the zōtl and gumper hogs and blood beetles and told me that you could teach me how to survive here. I'd really appreciate that."

"I'm sure you would," the wizan acknowledged. "But our ranks are closed. There are other human communities in the Werld. Rhene is a city where someone like you would be much happier."

"I would still prefer to stay here."

"Then you must demonstrate your usefulness to the Foke." The wizan's voice teetered on boredom. "What skills does a trader and a brewseller have?"

"I can learn."

"Tarfeather is not a school." The black bits of his eyes drilled Carl. "Can you make plastique? Can you ride the fallpath? Can you even tell time?" His eyes hooded, and he went into a rote routine: "As a wizan of the Foke, I find you unacceptable for inclusion in our ranks by reason of your inutility—"

"I can work," Carl objected. "I'll do labor."

"We all work, Carl," he explained, his voice a scaly integument. "There are no laborers. We share responsibility for labor equally."

"I'm sure I'm good for something." Carl didn't want to start off his new life by thwarting the eld skyle's will: He wanted the Foke to accept him. Allin was grinning lushly, and Carl knew that whatever pleased Allin was no good for him. "Is there a court of appeal?"

"No, my review is sufficient," the wizan replied in a voice of ravening flatness. "I order that you be taken directly to Rhene and traded for imprisoned Foke or sold for manufactured goods. Away—away."

Carl let himself be dragged out of the stall. Allin strode beside him, kicked him into a walk, and leered with satisfaction. The blue-robed guards followed to the exit.

"What is Rhene?" Carl asked at the doorway.

"You speak Foke and you don't know of Rhene?" He slapped Carl on the back and pushed him out of the wizan tent.

The beauty of the blued clouds and dark skyles had an unearthliness that made Carl shiver. "Is Rhene a prison city?"

Allin allowed himself a black laugh. "You were the reason my friends died, dropping. I'd just as soon imprison you as flay and gut you. But I am a Foke. We don't have penalties or prisons. Just exclusion."

He motioned Carl toward a steep trail that mounted a sinuous, reptilian terrain to the giant log moorings of a sky barge. The barge was a sleek wooden craft with a needle prow and furled black sail-fins.

"Rhene," Allin explained, "is a zōtl-built city for people—their favorite food. You might say it's a farm. Because it exists, we are spared the zōtl hunt."

"You said Rhene wasn't a prison," Carl reminded him.

"It isn't," he answered.

"Then what keeps the people inside?"

"The people are free to come and go. But going isn't really a hope for most of them." He gestured at the yawn of purpling sky and the skyles that cluttered space like motes of dust. "The cloudlanes, the fallpaths, and the skyles, *that* is the home of the Foke. But most of the people in Rhene would not survive to their next meal out here. They are content with their busy lives in the city. The zōtl androbs do most of the manual work and the people are free to cavort with one another. The only price they must pay is the lottery."

"I get a bad feeling from that word."

"When the zōtl need to feast, they conduct a lottery. The one percent who lose are eaten. If you survive seven lotteries, your name is permanently removed from the risk. Many people find the seven percent odds of losing more attractive than struggling for existence all the time out here. Isn't that really the way with you?"

They had come to the boarding ramp of the barge, where Foke bustled to load the hold with crates of blue cabbages. The sweet citron fragrance of the vegetable swirled in the air. Unbidden, the thought rose to Carl's mind that those were dream boles, a muscularly euphoric hallucinogen.

"There are great pleasures in the Werld," Allin said with a chill in his voice.

"Yeah, well, where I come from, the greatest pleasure is to be free."

Surprise ticked across Allin's face. He gripped Carl's beard and shook his head once. "Then why are you so obedient to fear?" He shoved Carl up the ramp. "Go on, get on board, dropping."

Carl boarded the ship and was steered by Allin's firm hand to a foredeck cabin. A dozen Foke sat on the benches that extended from the hull's ribs. They were conversing and staring out of the port visors at the scaffolding being slanted to slide the sky barge off the mountain and into the cloudy flightlanes. Allin and Carl sat with them until the barge jolted, tilted, and sledded into the sky.

"Do you know how this works?" Carl asked, after the barge had bucked violently and rocked into the steady sway of its cruise.

"Don't gad me with your questions, dropping." He swung to his feet. "Let's eat."

Carl's first full meal was braised cloud trout on a bed of butter-seared owlroot. He learned then that the Foke's fondest pleasure was eating. They were magical cooks and robust eaters. Their food was more diverse than anything he could remember of his older life.

That journey with Allin to Rhene lasted eighteen meals, no two alike, each almost supernaturally savory. During the flight, Carl learned enough about the Werld to actually think he might be happy in Rhene. The Foke were a dour, hardworking people, but they were convivial when they cooked or ate. Food, or course, was free, and all were happy to display their culinary skills for Carl, even though he was a dropping.

Not having Allin's reason for hating him, the Foke were indifferent to his origin and fate: Droppings were common. But praise among the Foke was not, and they were pleased by his laudations of their cooking prowess. Soon he was accepted among them.

Between meals, people slept casually and took turns helping with chores. Carl was started off cleaning latrines, but after his poetic praise of Foke cuisine had won him friends, he was relieved of the odious chores some of the time and allowed to work on deck.

The drunken sky, the winds motherly with grass scents and warm showers, powered glad feelings in him, and he affably did whatever he was told. Also, he had time to accustom himself to the seemingly endless depths of the Werld. Carl had always been nervous about heights and had avoided balcony seats, Ferris wheels, and plane trips. But after a while on deck, he was enthralled by the rhapsodies of distance, and his fear dwindled.

Knowledge came not only from what the eld skyle had given him but also from those around him. A kindly-face Foke physician taught him how to tell time. Units less than a week—twenty-five meals—did not officially exist; 5,555 "weeks" equaled one full rotation of the gravity rainbow that covered the Werld. The magnetic pole of the black hole, which was also the Rim, never varied in relation to the Werld, so with a compass one had a polar referent to watch the precession of the horizon's thin colors.

From other passengers, Carl learned that the zōtl were in firm command of the Werld, and that they allowed the Foke to exist in exchange for their regular harvest of dream boles. The boles sedated a large segment of the herd city's populace and made zōtl dominance easier to take and administer.

When the glass cupolas and silver minarets of Rhene appeared among the flamingo-tinted clouds, Carl was comfortable with the Foke way. Even Allin seemed less hostile. Carl had learned that Allin had been a free child—that is, he was raised in a tribal commune, a rougher life than the family children brought up by parents or other individuals. The Foke who had died helping Carl were the people he had grown up with. Carl's understanding of that resolved a lot of tension between them.

Rhene was a city of terraced skyles, monorails, and geometric domes opalescent as serpents' eyes. The undersides of these skyles were netted with nacreous flares and web lights, and Carl's first vista of the city had an ethereal effect on him. The air under the city glinted with the lights of individual flyers.

Carl had adjusted himself to his fate by this time, and he was eager to dock. Diatom-like flyers guided the barge into a colossal sky hangar of ribbon-contoured metal and moon-green spotlights. The Foke's wooden ship was primitive among the metal vessels honeycombing the dock, their shark bodies polished to black mirrors.

The technology amazed him. At the dock, androbs, squat mechanical stevedores, unloaded the holds. Scooters carried people across the wide marmoreal mall of androb-directed traffic to the clearing pavilion. Crystal parabolas arched through twenty stories of offices, coruscated with elevators and jewel-lighted rampways.

"How many people are here?" Carl wanted to know.

"In this part of the Werld, millions." Disdain manacled Allin's face. "This is a matter I wish to conduct as quickly as possible, dropping, so stop gawking and keep up with me."

Getting through the clearing pavilion was not as easy as Allin had expected. Queues of passengers and baggage-laden androbs clogged the waiting mall, and Allin grumbled impatiently to himself.

The mall, like everything Carl had seen in the Werld, was lush with natural vegetation. Green birds flitted through the trees that lined the rampways, and waterfalls clear as wind whirred between the levels, slapping among rockgardens where scarlet grass shuddered in a breeze of mist and mudscents. But the tameness, the precise order of the place, was disturbing after such a long journey through the wild spaces.

Carl was gaping with apprehension at this city woven into the terrain when he noticed a woman standing at the lower level on a path among red and blue algal pools. She was a long, coltish woman in a black-and-coral shift. And she was staring at him.

That was not unusual, actually, since he was ganglier and ruddier than everyone else. But she wasn't goggling at him so much as looking for recognition from him. A tribal crowd carrying seedheads mounted on whip poles swept by her, blue birds flashing about them. After they had passed, she was gone.

Allin was seated on the androb in line ahead of

him, his concrete-colored eyes glazed over. Carl watched tiny, blue-bottomed mandrills prowl a brake of bamboo and reminisced nostalgically about Manhattan, where waiting in line was a way of life. He slept awhile among the baggage on the androb behind him, dreamed erotically of confronting Sheelagh with his new body and of her tugging at his clothes. He woke to find himself being stripped by coilringed metallic tentacles.

Carl howled and writhed, and Allin's big hand clapped onto his shoulder. "Ease up, dropping." His voice glinted with humor, and Carl knew then something unpleasant was going to happen. "This is your medical exam. It's required before I can sell you."

They were in a tiny room of flower-twined partitions, a padded slant table, and the green glaring lens of the tentacled ceiling. All of Carl's orifices were probed, blood was drawn from his arm, skin scraped from his abdomen, and the hair shaved from his face.

He saw himself in the androb's chrome surface, and again he didn't know himself. The face staring back at him was longboned and pugnacious.

Silk-textured garments tailored for his precise dimensions emerged from a wall panel. They were a white tunic shirt, loose black trousers, and corded leather sandals.

Carl dressed and was led by Allin around the blossomed partition to a garishly lit chamber, reminiscent of a SoHo art gallery. A group of a dozen people stared at him and began a swift numerical exchange. He was being sold.

The bargaining went quickly. Within moments, a bald and sinewy little man was clasping to Carl's wrist a sturdy strap attached to a thickly corded leash. The leash was metal-clamped to his belt.

Allin was pleased. "You've earned Tarfeather enough fiber cord for another counsel tent and two tree homes."

"That much?" Carl peered into his owner's coria-
ceous face. "What makes me worth anything to you? I
don't have any skills. You haven't even interviewed me."

He looked at Carl distrustfully and then at Allin.
"Doesn't he know?"

"You'll be taking the place of Picwah's son in the
lottery," Allin informed Carl with his pyknic leer, "as
well as working as his servant for one tenth of a cycle.
After that, if you're still alive, you're free."

"Thanks."

"As part of the deal," Allin added, "I promised
your lord Picwah that if you caused him any trouble I
would cut off your ears." He grinned like a wolf. "You
know, of course, I'd have traded you to the zōtl themselves for a Foke. It's your fortune that the last prisoners
were taken on to Galgul before we arrived. Farewell,
dropping. Work hard."

Picwah snapped at Carl's wrist leash. "Come on—I
have much to do."

"Wait!" The command cracked from across the
gallery through the veils of muttering from other ne-
gotiations.

Carl heard it and looked. Picwah didn't and kept
going. His leash jerked taut against Carl's immobility,
and the scrawny man was yanked to his haunches.

"Are you acting up already?" he almost-screamed,
popping to his feet and glaring at Carl.

Carl thumbed his attention to the approaching
figures. The woman he had seen earlier by the algal
pools was rushing across the chamber. In her wake
were two blue-robed, wide-bodied Foke.

"A wizan," Allin noted and dutifully bowed.

The fragrance of rose madder accompanied her as
she stepped up to Carl, her gray-streaked eyes flecked
with redgold regarding him as if his face were a mirror.

Carl played his gaze over her oak-brown hair and

the lynx angles of her face. "Evoë," he guessed in a wishful whisper.

Surprise swung across her face. "I do know you," she breathed back. "But from where?"

The guards were watching her with anxiety. "How do you know her personal name?" one of them queried Carl.

"My lady, you are distressed," the other said to her. "We should go."

She touched Carl's arm, and a blur of energy warmed him. "Why are you here?" she asked.

Carl held up his strapped wrist. "I've been sold." He cast a nod to Allin. "By him."

She looked hard at Allin. "Why are you selling him? He looks Foke-worthy."

Allin met her stare with a stern countenance. "He has been wizan-appraised, my lady." The Foke warrior observed the wizan guards' edginess, and he asked: "What has distressed you?"

Evoë said nothing, for she was watching Carl for what was familiar.

"The last of her kin, a distaff aunt, was a prisoner in Rhene," a guard related. "We had come with the ransom to free her. But she has already been taken to Galgul."

That last word cracked the guard's voice. Allin nodded in sympathy to their anxiety. "You are indeed distressed, my lady," he said loudly to her; then, to the guards: "You must take her to where she can rest."

"Will you came with me?" Evoë asked Carl.

His heart was squashed with feeling. The eld skyle had been right about this woman—she was all the colors of waking to him, the flesh of dreams. She wasn't shimmeringly beautiful or vein-poundingly erotic. But her slender face enthralled him with its waif eyes and a

puckish smile that showed small white teeth. What
could he say? He loved the melody of her features.

The guards took her arms and she shrugged them
off. "Will you come with me?" she asked again, more
urgently.

"Yes," Carl's whole body said.

"Lady!" Allin barked. "We have witnesses to your
distress. I am hereby overriding your authority by Foke
right for the Foke good."

The guards seized her. She slumped and twisted,
throwing herself against one guard for purchase and
heaving the other to the ground. With her free arm,
she jabbed viperlike at the remaining guard's face, and
she was free. Her hand reached into the guard's robe,
and she came away with a pistol.

Allin had settled into an attack crouch, and he
crabbed toward her, ignoring the gun.

With both hands, Carl grabbed Picwah by his
shirtfront, hoisted him into the air, and flung him at
Allin.

A knifeblade grinned in Evoë's hand. She cut the
leash, and she and Carl bolted for the chamber's exit.
They ran through gold-lighted corridors and into a
transparent elevator. The lift tugged at their tensed
insides, and as the gallery level pulled off, they both
laughed with relief.

"My name's Carl." He took her hand, and the
warm electricity was still there.

"In my whole span, nothing like this has ever
happened to me before." Her face glowed apricot from
the exertion. "How do you know my name?"

"The same way I know your language. They were
the gifts of an eld skyle."

"How long have you been in the World?"

"About twenty or so meals."

The elevator stopped, and she guided Carl out by

his hand. They were on a rooftop. Clouds the color of gunsmoke wisped overhead. Below, a laser-lit city blazed like magma.

"Rhene," Evoë announced. "The City of Sacrifice. We can't stay here."

The wind was steep on the top ramp of the clearing pavilion, and Carl was sure she was going to jump to the fallpath. His heart was galloping in anticipation. She led him instead along the curve of the ramp in the circle of a landing pad. Dozens of glossy, enameled flyers were parked along the perimeter.

Evoë selected a blue-toned one and raised its blackglass canopy. "Get in."

The sling Carl crawled into held his weight and swiveled wildly until he realized he had the control grip in his left hand. Evoë slid into the second sling, and the faceted blackglass hood closed with a sigh from its airtight bolts. The interior was black. Green points tapped on in the dark as Evoë activated its drive.

"Are we stealing this thing?" Carl asked into the blackness.

"It's a flyer," the answer arrived with a chorus of moving control lights and audial cues, "and any citizen of Rhene may fly it."

The canopy's blackglass phased to transparency, and Carl watched with glittering fascination as the landing pad dropped away and they were suddenly high over Rhene. The clearing pavilion, he saw at once, was the city of glass towers that he had seen from afar during his thornwing flight. In the direction toward where he had been then, clouds folded in on themselves like the interior of a brain.

"That's the Cloudgate," Evoë's alto voice informed him. "It's the only safe route through the destroyer winds to the Welkyn where the zōtl live. That's why

Rhene is here—to guard their upper World from the human animals they breed in Midwerld for their food."

"I came through there in a thornwing."

"That's about the only way through," Evoë agreed. "The fallpath flows down. Thornwings can get down the Cloudpath, but not up it. The only way up is a flyer. And the zōtl destroy all unauthorized craft."

Rhene glowered below them like embers. "Where are we going?"

"Where no one will find us." She made some small adjustments and leaned back in her sling.

Skyles whirled past as their flyer swiftly found its way through the maze of the World. The continuous abrupt changes in direction never touched them, and they hung gracefully in their slings.

Evoë was looking at Carl with an earnestness in her dolphin-tinted eyes that gave him the same slick feeling as luck. "Tell me about yourself," she requested, "so that maybe I can figure out why I feel this way about you."

"What way?"

A burr of anxiety snagged her voice: "Don't you feel it?"

He did. The eld skyle had prepared him for it, and it still amazed him. The sublime tranquillity of a summer afternoon prismed all his thoughts and feelings. He had been saturated with strangeness since he had been snatched out of his former life—and now the luster of caring emotion welling in him, the most natural and primal emotion of any child, seemed strangest of all. "I'm in love."

They laughed a lot during that flight. The tight space of that pod seemed as big and full of promise to Carl as the entire room of May. He told her about himself. Not everything, of course. He left out his balding head and flat feet. But he told her the highlights: St. Tim's, college, the brokerage house in Manhattan, and the Blue Apple. He was surprised by how little there was. And how interested she was in it.

Evoë never finished her story. She was one and a half cycles old and had completed many initiations. She had been born into an ancient Foke clan with a legacy of fealties to other clans. That meant she had spent half of her first cycle serving and learning from various and scattered Foke tribes. She had attained a great deal. Her most valuable lesson was learning to surrender the leadership role she had been born to. Over the years of her ancestral servitude, when she cleaned the lodges and reared the children of other noble clans, she was immersed in and fell in love with the simpleness of living. After her thrall was over, she stayed close to that love, and she lived longer than any other in her family. She was the first wizan in their known history. And that had been a great humiliation to her clan.

Among the Foke, wizan were honored. They were allowed to write books. But warrior leaders, chiefs, were glorified. They alone could carry the guns smithied in the Foke's secret armories. The two were never found together in one person, though Chief Wizan was a popular character in Foke myth and lore. Foke chiefs were bound by law to take the Foke's greatest risks, and they always led in battle. None ever lived more than half a cycle.

Evoë suspended the telling of her story when the flyer landed on a skyle cliff among spires of fir. The pod went black.

"We'll send the flyer back," her soft voice said in the darkness. "They'll only be able to trace us to here—and by the time they do, we'll be long gone. Here, take this." She handed him the gun she had taken from her guard. "I have one, too. And some naphthal pods—firebombs. I had come to Rhene armed, to free my kin."

Carl took the gun and tucked it in his belt.

The canopy bolts hissed open, and sharp alpine air flushed in. Carl rolled out of the flyer and stood up among bleached grass drooping over a whispering plunge. His eyes looked like raisins, and Evoë sang with laughter. "Don't worry. I'm not going to lose you now," she said before shoving him into space.

They fell a hundred meters before the fallpath caught them firmly, and with her arm around him, they rose toward clouds red and blue as bruises. They flew through the bucketing wind a far spell before they launched into a calm warm flow where they could talk. The giant terrain rivered by on all sides. They kept themselves positioned so that the dark Rim side was above them, and they could look down into the glimmering reaches of the Eld. She continued her story, and Carl learned about the World.

Evoë had lived in Rhene for over a quarter of a cycle, and she knew the intensities of pleasure that kept people there. The zōtl had developed the bliss collar, a rapture device that magnetically stimulated the limbic brain and wove the cellular quilt of the body with pleasure while leaving the mind clear. Like almost everyone in Rhene, she had worn the bliss collar, and she never cared then that her name was in the lottery or that people she knew had lost and been taken to Galgul.

She had survived all seven drawings and probably would still be wearing the collar if she hadn't witnessed a Foke attack. She saw only the end of it, after the insurgents had already succeeded in blasting their way through the barriers of the Well, the prison where people were gathered before being sent on to Galgul. The prisoners had already been freed, and she'd seen their flyers falling down the sky away from the incandescence of Rhene. To cover their escape, a band of Foke had stayed behind and held off the androbs with a commandeered laser cannon.

Evoë had stood on the cordon line with the crowd and cheered as the attack squad of androbs was shattered by the blinding bolts from the cannon. After the prisoners were well gone, the Foke guerrillas dispersed. But by then, the zōtl had arrived.

She had never seen the zōtl before. They came in their own flyers, designed for their alien anatomies. Their flyers were man-long needles that cut through the air almost faster than seeing and could stop or shift direction instantly. Within moments, they had stunned all of the guerrillas still in Rhene, and they carried them up the Cloudgate and into Galgul.

The Foke had lost seven fighters and had freed over a hundred prisoners. The sacrifice and the victory profoundly affected Evoë, and shortly afterward she left Rhene and returned to the wilds. The last half cycle, she had been traveling among the Foke clans, living again their nomadic rituals.

While she spoke, Evoë modified the way Carl held his limbs so that he was more comfortable with the sensation of freefalling and rising with the vallations of space. Foke as experienced as Evoë could read the flightlanes in the stream curves of clouds and the shapes of skyles. What had looked to Carl to be a mere moiling of clouds among the suspended jumble of skyles began to take on the continuity and direction of a terrain as she talked. He also learned to tell at a distance the warm skyles and clouds from the cold by the flowlines of the wind.

Evoë guided them toward a skyle and held him by

his belt as they broke free of the fallpath with strong bodytwists. Gravity steepened at once, and he would have hit the approaching rock ledge with his face if Evoë hadn't righted him at the last moment.

They ate owlroots and slamsteaks. The slamsteak was a large snail found on some skyles. The Foke ricocheted the snail off the fallpath so that it slammed back into the rocks hard enough to break its sturdy shell. Braised and seasoned with local herbs, it was tender as lobster and sapid as filet mignon.

They jumped from skyle to skyle eating as they went and working on Carl's blundering flying skills. When Carl had worn out his anxiety about jumping and landing and he was familiar enough with the sky geography to begin to see the fallpaths among the clouds and floating mountains, they landed to rest.

Lying together on their backs with clouds building into great treeshapes, violet and yellow, and the trees themselves cloudlike, their branches boiling in the green wind, Carl was happy. Maybe it was the first time in his life that he was happy. Or maybe he'd just never been awake enough to notice it when it had happened before. But he was so happy that he could hear a song playing inside him that he'd never heard before.

Carl had never been musically inclined, yet that interior melody was vivid enough for him to hum. Evoë reached into the coral-stitched pocket of her black robe and took out a devil's harp, a blond wood instrument with small internal windbags and pipes. She caught his tune and chivvied it in the wind with the rustling branches and the hickett of tree toads. It was the first and simplest song he had ever created, and it was stamped with the common melodic traits of his time on earth:

Carl wanted Evoë. Her smile was mist in the soft shadows, and her fawn-colored hair, plaited and clasped with red snailshells, smelled of leafsmoke. Bleached skulls of rodents glared in the heat-stunted grass where the hawks had dropped them. And Evoë played her lucid music, giggling and empty-headed with their joy.

She took off her black robe, put aside her holstered gun and belt of naphthal pods, and was left wearing a body-clinging chemise. Carl gawped at her loveliness, the curves of her breasts and thighs luminous with sunburn, and then caught himself and focused on the rootweave of the nearest tree. For a while, he shifted his gaze from the jazz of her laughter-shimmying breasts to the pointillism of blue-and-green trees—from the shadow of pubic hair behind the hem of her chemise to the slow mandala of a dew-spider in the shaded grass. Her heart bobbed like a cork.

They touched each other at the crest of the right moment, and silks of feeling tickled the spaces of hunger inside them. The taste of her salt skin mingled with the power turning within, and everything loosened, splintered, multiplied.

When they made love, they became each other. She felt his brimming strength, the magnetism in his bones, and she saw herself as if through his eyes backsprawled in a ruffle of grass and horsemint. His eyes closed, and he felt the gorging magic filling him like light, tightening through the lens of his awareness to the burning focus of an orgasm. The resin smell of crushed grass spelled over them.

Solitudes opened, and they rocked back into their own bodies, the sex between them liquid, filling the dark gnarled foot of the tree with a charmed, fleece odor.

Her limbs were straggled, sticky, humming with dreams. She held to his arms, and the glittering sounds of their bodies and the surge of feeling in the nimbus of their flesh opened her completely to the moment: She felt the slippery green moss floating out of the treeroot beneath her, and the other skyles iced with the Werld light, sun-high, swelling the tree bark, rising the sap.

A claret light sheened among the clouds when they came out of each other. She had seen through him, beyond his adamized body and past life on earth to the cryptic silence in him. Carl didn't know how else to explain it. He felt that they had interpenetrated each other's souls. They had heard each other's stories—now they felt each other's inner life.

He remembered the eld skyle telling him about Evoë, and how she would be mated to him by the very molecular nature of his body. And he was at peace. He knew this woman truly loved him just for him. She lay across his warm chest, and the smell of her hair reminded him of rain. How could the eld skyle have known? Was it telepathy that it had used to select Evoë for him? The moment was too wonderful for him to think that thought through. The light was ripe, the rock shadows somnolent. Later, he would wonder why he had accepted his new life so mindlessly. Several lizardwings flicked through the plum sky like meteors.

They roamed for what seemed a lifetime. The skyles fed them and the fallpath carried them. They visited clan sites and mingled with the Foke, but they never went to Tarfeather. There was too much else to see for them to return to the moving capital and perhaps provoke Allin and his clan's wizan with the fact of Carl's freedom. They had sentenced him to slavery, though he bore no grudge against them; their rejection, after all, had sent him to Rhene and Evoë. He was not eager to confront them again.

Among the wet, cloudbroomed skyles in a far corner of the Werld, they met a wizan clan that specialized in Werld knowledge. They were the closest thing to scientists Carl had met among the Foke. They had no hardware, none of the apparatus he associated with science. They were not technicians. They were, rather, historians, pooling and recording the knowledge of droppings like himself. What they learned was preserved in books that they published with their own presses.

Next to food, the written language was adored by

the Foke. Everyone read and wrote, and each clan had its own press. Because of the difficulty of obtaining materials, only wizan were freely published. Others had to work hard for the right. Religious tomes and cookbooks were the most common publication. But Foke were also fond of journals and treatises.

Carl and Evoë met the scientific wizan at the Cloudwall. That was far across the Werld, on the blue side, at the apparent perimeter. The clouds piled up there into a virtual wall that no one had ever penetrated because the Werld literally ended there. The wizan had gathered in this place not so much to study the Cloudwall as to stay hidden from the zōtl. They were compiling a New History of the Werld, and they needed the obscuring mists of the Cloudwall to cover their operation.

Carl was surprised by how much the wizan knew of the universe. The Werld was self-contained, yet generations of contact with droppings dating back to their own origins one hundred and fifty cycles ago had revealed a fairly accurate depiction of the cosmos. They were happy to see Carl, for he spoke their language and could more easily relate what he had learned. There was, however, little he could add to their understanding.

The wizan knew the universe was closing up. They were the last human age, and that knowledge spurred their mystical pursuits: The meaning of life, for the wizan, was meaning itself—the discovery or, when necessary, the invention of meaning. They believed that all creation was light and light's gradients, and so all beings, to them, were equal. The Werld was clement enough and big enough to sustain this philosophy. Foke communities made up the rules they chose to live by, and individuals unhappy with the collective were free to leave and find or start cummunities more to their liking.

The wizan were appalled by Carl's stories of earth:

Old age, disease, prison, and human-slaughtering war were horrors alien to the Foke way. In the telling, Carl amazed himself at having endured life on earth. Compared to the Werld, even with the zōtl and gumper hogs, earth was a synonym for hell.

Among the wizan, living from meal to meal in their simple routines, unashamed of time, Carl was grateful to be free of his past, all the incomprehensions and indecisions of existing at the ass end of earth's most violent millennium. He was free. He had been delivered from a madness that he had once thought was all there was. And now here he was, in a world of secret places, bonded to a woman he loved. Life was good.

Evoë, too, was caught up in Carl's happiness. Her life since meeting him had been a continuous surprise of feeling. She had loved before and had reared children, but she had lost them all to zōtl and the wild things of the Werld. Death's indirections had long ago liberated her from love—until now. Black memory faded before the brilliance of her lover's smile. He made her feel strong with life. His touch pried her loose from herself, and his embrace carried her loneliness. She would die before she would let herself lose him.

Carl and Evoë's time among the sapient and gentle wizan of the Cloudwall left them peaceful and not as guarded as the dangers of the Werld demanded. During their long journeying, they had witnessed both the wonders and the hostilities of the skyles. Sickness was practically unheard-of, as the eld skyle had foretold, and no one aged beyond his full maturity. Yet the Werld's population was relatively scant. The treacheries of the fallpath crippled and killed many Foke all the time. Certain magnetic skyles were renowned for the healing of bones, and Carl had spent some time there himself with a snapped wrist. Other skyles, especially the larger ones, were lethal with the presence of predators. But the greatest risk to Foke life was the zōtl raid.

The zōtl used the radar in their nimble needle-craft to fly through the clouds that spiraled the length of the Werld. The only safe place for Foke along the Cloudriver was beside the Wall. The wizan told Carl that gavitational fluctuations along the Wall had destroyed many a zōtl craft, and the paineaters rarely flew there now.

When Evoë and Carl left the wizan, they traveled on the fog-tattered fringe of the Wall until they came to where it joined the Cloudriver and they had to move inward. No Foke could travel in the Cloudriver for very long. Vision was an empty lilac-gray, and one had to gauge the fallpath by feel alone. Landing anywhere was out of the question. Not only were those cloudforest skyles evil with bizarre predators, but there was no sure way to catch the fallpath. The visual clues were not there. One had to jump into the wind and pray.

So Carl and Evoë stayed above the clouds, looking for a well of clear space and lighted skyles that tunneled through the Cloudriver. The fringe was a tricky place, since the wind could suddenly shift and smother the fallpath and nearby skyles with blinding clouds.

Just that was happening to them, as it had happened numerous times before. Cauliflowering clouds loomed out of the Cloudriver, billowing purple and gold. Around them, rain girandoled, a gray halo sheeting the flowlines of the fallpath and smoking over the skyles.

They soared toward a flower-bright skyle where heat shimmered in the cup of a small valley. When Carl glanced back to gauge the advance of the cloudfall, he saw them, and it was already too late.

They had hidden in the Cloudriver and had approached with the blossoming clouds until they were close enough to strike. Carl thought in that first instant that they were Foke. They were human, and all six wore finsuits. But in the next instant, he realized they were moving too fast for Foke. He noticed the black thrusters on their backs the same moment Evoë spotted them.

Without hesitation, she unsnapped a naphthal pod from the belt under her robe and flung it toward them. The fireball caught one of the flyers head-on and splashed with the impact, searing two others. All three whirled out of control and spun flapping flames into the cathedral buttes of a skyle.

The remaining three were already too close for another naphthal pod, and Carl unholstered his gun. He never even had the chance to aim. Evoë glanced about and saw a steep-banking plunge in the fallpath below them. She grabbed Carl in both of her arms and pulled him close.

"Carl, I love you," she said, and her face was a blaze of feeling, her soul leaning against the opal light in her eyes. "Stay alive."

He burbled the beginning of some reply, and she twisted him about, tripped him with a swing of her legs, and toppled him into the drop of the fallpath that sheared away from them. Carl was too clumsy to stop or even slow his fall. He watched Evoë distance away.

The three flyers were almost on her. One of them peeled off to pick Carl up, and Evoë drew her gun and fired several rounds, her body wrenching with the coil of each shot.

Then the two flyers were on her, and she was bowled over, snagged by their grapnels, and swung away.

Carl jerked about to see his pursuer rolling lifelessly in a cloud of his blood. Trying to brake himself, Carl went into a roll. He tumbled head over heels in a freefall and was soon lost among the skyles whipping past him like freights.

Panic hardened to clarity, and he utilized the techniques Evoë had been teaching him to slow a fall. He pulled his finsuit sleekly against him before carefully unfurling its fins to cup the air. His fall relaxed to a float, and he swam toward the contraflow that always paralleled a fallpath.

The contraflow was there, and he swooped back toward Evoë. He swung around the obstructing skyles in time to see the two pirates carrying her limp body away.

He'd lost his gun in the fall, but that's not why he hung back. Emerging from the Cloudriver was the black chevron of a jumpship. He watched helplessly as they boarded and the jumpship slinked back into the colossal clouds.

Carl raged. His blood sang with despair, and he howled at the Cloudriver, dashing in and out of its blankness hoping to be taken by the pirates and joined again, at least in fate, with his Evoë.

They were gone.

Carl was alone, staring into the long emptiness of his life.

In the end, there was only one place for him to go. If Evoë was imprisoned in Rhene, he couldn't hope to free her. And if she was in Galgul, an army couldn't save her. At the end of his hysterics and his heroic and fatalistic strategies, only one hope remained. The eld skyle.

He journeyed eldward, stopping only for the sustenance he needed to travel. His sleep-frayed alertness went into rage-drive, automatically guiding him through the brightening heights toward the feathery radiance of the Welkyn. Only after he saw the rainbows threading the glass minarets of Rhene did he seek a brambly covert and sleep.

He nightmared Evoë's abduction and woke sick with anguish. His pain led him finally to the slow whorl of the Gate, the down-moving fallpath that was the only entrance to the Welkyn. Claws of frustration tore his insides as he circled the vast area, hunting a way up the gravity slope.

Carl lay spraddled in a field of golden grass among bells of green flowers, charred inside from his thwarted approaches. His grimaced mind was contemplating the madness of entering Rhene alone for a flyer when he saw a brown tumbleweed rolling toward him across the meadow.

Its tangled form unwrapped as it approached, wobbling into a wreath of tufted vines, and finally stopped ten paces away and lifting to its full stature. It was a thornwing, a crumpled mass of thistly, snarled twine with a tiny hooked head at the crest of its amorphous shape. Long talons flexed on the ends of its two thickest vines. By the bright-green scar that creased its back, Carl knew it was the thornwing that had carried him and that Allin had wounded.

"How did you find me?" Carl asked with a jubilation that sat him up. "How could you know?"

It stared back with the dark clarity of a shoeshine.

As Carl stood up, one of its arm-thick vines rose above the golden grass. Carl went over to it and let it coil itself about him. His feet eased off the ground as the creature hugged him to itself and began its loping run. The golden grass blurred beneath them, and they leaned upward against the air.

The gold-and-blue meadow pulled back to a glint near the top of a ravine-haggard skyle as they caught the lift of an outward-bound fallpath.

The Cloudgate's iridescent clouds filled half the

visible World, a vast sea anemone of thunderheads flicking lightning near its black mouth. They flew directly for that center. Below and behind them, skyles sparkled like charms, bright with the delicate and luminous structures of Rhene. Jumpships and flyers dusted the vast interstices with the continual flow of their movement.

The thornwing rolled, and Rhene slipped from sight. The air went cool as ether, and Carl saw only cliffs of stormcloud splintered with lightning. He stilled himself, awaiting guidance from an inner voice, a telepathic link with the thornwing or the eld skyle that was guiding it.

Nothing.

Its body shuddered with the strain of its flight. The rush of wind strengthened, a wind blue with the scent of lightning. And in the distance, the howling began.

They slashed in and out of the clouds, and Carl closed his eyes against the wind-teasing sight. The cry of the wind sharpened to a screech. He knew by that sound of ripping metal that they were at the neck of the Cloudgate where the shear winds were closest to becoming a garroting whirlpool.

The sound of the screaming winds sluicing through their arteries of gravity knotted in Carl's brain with the struggle of the thornwing. It was heaving itself upward through the soldering cold like a salmon.

By arching his head, Carl could see its head, the black diamonds of its eyes clasped with intensity. His insides cramped with the joltiness of the flight, stalling before the metallic shriek of the Cloudgate.

A jumpship slid by fifty meters away, its engines spinning flames like a furnace. The thornwing twisted and unsprang into a mighty lurch, and Carl's heart almost pulled free of his ribs. The devil whistle of the wind muted as they caught the wake of the jumpship's ascent.

The thornwing hurtled with acceleration, riding the drag wind of the large craft. Its grip slackened with its acceptance of the lift, and Carl slid low enough in its coiled grip to see beyond the skeletal frame of the thornwing to the vista looming ahead.

The clouds on all sides brailed into azure radiance, and the whirlpool of the tearing winds opened into a luminous cornucopia. The jumpship tipped away, and they caught the drift of a fallpath through the bright ring of the Cloudgate and into the glare of the Welkyn.

Far off along the wheel of Carl's sight, black spheres clotted the spaces among the skyles. That was Galgul. The atmosphere around it was soiled with the vapors steaming from the seams of the City of Pain.

The blood banging in his skull drummed louder with the thought that Evoë could already be in the alien city, suffering. His tension was conveyed to the thornwing, and its grip squeezed more snugly. The charge in the air from their passage through the Cloudgate flickered bluely on the thorntips of the creature, crackling as it spun away from Galgul, strong as a shout.

Carl had known from the instant he recognized the thornwing that it would take him to the eld skyle that had reshaped his life, and his soul was a ferment of questions, rage, and pain. But the Welkyn calmed him.

The silvery light smashing against the feather-braided clouds was entirely different from the dusky cloud towers of Midwerld. Rainbows sheeted the spaces between skyles, and even the undersides of the forested asteroids were bright with ambient light.

The return journey to the eld skyle turned his thoughts back to his first flight through the Welkyn. He had been smallminded then, unready for the marvelous, a fool of the unexpected. And he saw then that in his despair for Evoë he had almost wholly returned to his clangorous selfishness. That insight dispelled his anguish, and he returned to his staring senses.

Carl hung in the thornwing's sky alert as a hawk, studying the wilderness of skyles drifting by. All at once, vision jumped. His whole body flinched, though their flight was smooth. He didn't understand what he'd experienced, until it happened again some long while later. While he was following the forest pattern of a skyle, it vanished in an eyeblink and he was seeing a new panorama. He hadn't passed out. He had passed through.

A word trembled into his awareness. *Lynk*. He'd heard the word before in conversation with wizan. Lynks were corridors that connected far-apart points in the Werld. Midwerld had few lynks, and that's why Carl hadn't thought much of it before. The language-instilled knowledge informed him that the Welkyn became more and more populated with lynks near the eld. The topmost lynks were the ones of the eld skyles used to plant their spores in other universes, for the outmost lynks connected with the cosmic stream through the center of the ring singularity. But here in the Welkyn, the lynks interconnected. Somehow the thorn-wing knew how to find the lynks that would take them to one specific eld skyle among the millions.

Not long after this understanding, Carl recognized the dolmen slabs of rock squaring the shape of the eld skyle that had re-created him. The thornwing dangled him out over the dragon-long lake, and he saw himself cliff-faced, bearded and rugged as a Viking in the water's slick surface before it dropped him.

The water was hot. It seared his eyeseams and earholes and stung his lips. He held his breath and curled into an upward stroke. But he wasn't rising. The water that he remembered as being firmly buoyant was pressing him down.

His held breath went stiff in his throat and skewered the back of his mouth. He retched with the impulse to breathe, his arms and legs flailing for the air. But down he went. And soon after the glaring pain in his eyesockets vapored into nervelight, the last of his breath spurted out of him and the hot fluid of the skyle pierced his body.

His horror squealed with pain. All sensation, every pinpoint cell of him, squeezed out its agony. And he went dead.

Nothing.

Then darkness healing to the darkest blue.

"Welcome back, Carl," the solemn voice of the eld skyle sounded through him. Its familiarity struck him alert in the deaf-and-dumbness.

"I see you've changed a great deal within yourself," it noted, and Carl gleamed with the affection he heard there.

"Eld skyle?" Carl thought with all the mental power he could focus through his dead-stillness.

"Not so loud."

"Sorry," Carl responded reflexively. "Eld skyle—am I glad to see you."

"Because you think I can help you recover your beloved Evoë—is that right?"

"Can't you?"

"Of course. That's why I had you returned to me. I am, I told you, a five-space consciousness. I know your needs better than you do."

Carl felt like a lab animal, floating in stillness, stripped to the flatness of his life. He glowed with relief. "It's good to be back. But I can't stay long. Evoë's been taken away from me by the zōtl. They could be pain-sowing her now."

"Not yet. But soon."

"Eld skyle—please, help me." Carl's desperation flared before the blankness of his suspension quashed it.

"I need you, too, Carl."

The absurdity of that thought dumbfounded Carl. "For what? You're a five-space consciousness."

"But I can't move in three-space. You must move for me."

Carl hung silent, becalmed with curiosity.

"I need your full and absolute cooperation in this venture." Its voice went still as the hum of an electrical storm. "You do indeed have free will, Carl Schirmer. And if you misuse it now, you could destroy a world. Your world."

Carl missed two beats. "Earth?"

"Then you do remember earth? It certainly remembers you. ZeeZee thinks of you quite often. Your abrupt departure has had a profound effect on him. You recall, he was a scientist. Well, what spoor you left behind before coming here has forced him to some very cutting conclusions."

"Zee—" Carl's soul squirmed. "That's the past, eld skyle. I need your help now, with Evoë."

"You're also frequently in Caitlin Sweeney's thoughts," the eld skyle continued, heedless of Carl. "You were her friend, her one real friend, lost devilishly, taken in an ungodly way into the Unknown. Her drink has gotten the best of her now, and the Blue Apple is about to be closed. Sheelagh can't run it without you."

Those names jolted Carl like blows. "I don't want to go back to them. What are you talking about?"

"You are going back, Carl. I need something, and I want you to get it for me."

"What is it?"

"Three point five tonnes of pig manure."

A zest of levity sparkled through Carl. "Three point five tonnes of pig manure," he echoed.

"Yes, Carl. That is the medicine I need to survive. My ecology is off. I've been toxifying for over a century now, and you're the first one to come through me with the chance of helping me. I need to introduce a certain kind of organism, a bacterium, that will redress my biokinesis and stop my body's degradation. That organism does not exist in the Werld. But it does on earth—in pig manure."

"And Evoë?"

"If you get me the pig manure, I'll help you get her back from the zōtl."

"There's not enough time."

"No, Carl. You are wrong. Here in the Werld, there is all the time there ever was. I have the means to return you to earth for as long as is necessary, then bring you back here in only moments of Werld time."

Carl's mind prickled with thoughts. "Why are you telling me all this about pig manure now? Why didn't you just send me for it when I first arrived?"

"And not introduce you to Evoë? Risk your staying on earth and leaving me here alone, sick and dying? No, I had to be sure you would return."

In the gust of the moment, all emotion cooled in Carl. He went calm as a storm-eye. Maybe the eld skyle had shifted his blood chemistry, he thought.

"Blood physics," the eld skyle corrected. "Chemistry is molecule-size physics. Biology is human-size physics. Astronomy is galaxy-size physics."

"Okay—okay. Are you jerking me around or not?"

"If I were not modulating your blood physics you'd be hollowed out with horror now."

"Try me."

"Don't tempt me."

A kelpy feeling wavered in Carl's stomach, hurrying toward nausea. "Stop it," Carl cried. "You've made your point."

The axle of calm returned, and the queasiness passed.

Unhampered by emotion, Carl's fatefulness looked geometric. "What do you want me to do?" he asked.

"Listen to me very carefully," the voice responded darkly. "You will be endowed with powers more subtle and direct than anything your kind have known. Consider this: Where has everything come from? The calcium in your bones, the oxygen in your brain? All the nuclei of your body more complex than hydrogen were forged in the thermonuclear furnaces of stars that twinkled ten to the ninth years before you were born. And the hydrogen of those ancient stars and all the subnuclear particles that exist everywhere in the universe—where are they from?"

"The Hamptons. What do I know?"

"They are remnants of the most violent event of all—the gravitational collapse at the beginning of time. The radiation universe to which your body and mine belong is the shed skin of a living process bigger than universes. What you know as inertia is the most direct physical link you have with this metareality."

"And I thought I was an orphan."

"Have you ever thought about inertia? Few humans have, and then only briefly. There isn't much for a human of your time to think. The best minds of your history had only begun to suspect that inertia reflects the profound unity of the cosmos. What keeps matter at rest or in uniform motion in the same straight line unless some external force acts on it? When you take a hairpin turn, what *is* the force that pulls you to the side? Your scientists believed it was all the distant matter in the universe constraining movement. The All acting on the Part."

"What has this got to do with Evoë *or* pig manure?"

"As a scientist of your time, Niels Bohr, said: 'A great truth is a truth whose opposite is also a great truth.' The Part can act on the All. Here in the World there are beings, far from human, who have mastered inertial principles much as your species controlled electromagnetic laws. They are Rimstalkers, and, as their name implies, they dwell in the World's dark zone, Rataros, near the Rim. They are the ones, as my allies, who will provide the technology for our venture."

"Okay, already. Give me the details."

"They will give you a portable lynk that you will use to transport the manure here, to me. The thornwings will help me distribute it. The lynk they will give you is nine centimeters long, five wide, and two thick. Very easy to hide. Bury it in the mounds of manure. It will take ten weeks to inertially convert three point five tonnes of manure, and during that time you must protect it. The lynk won't be vulnerable to your fellow humans. It has a field projector in it that will make it impenetrable to all human devices. But the zōtl have a radiation technology sophisticated enough to disrupt the field and destroy the lynk."

"There are no zōtl on earth," Carl told the eld skyle.

"There will be while you're there. The inertial displacement of your lynk will almost certainly be detected by the zōtl scanner in Galgul. Your lynk, for the ten weeks that it is operating, will be an open corridor between the World and earth. Not just zōtl can follow it to earth but any of the creatures here in the World who might accidentally pass through the World's lynk maze."

"Isn't that a bit risky for earth and the four billion like me there? I mean, the zōtl have needlecraft and laser cannon—and they eat us. Isn't there some other—safer—way to get your pig manure?"

"The danger is greater even than the zōtl," the eld skyle said gloomily. "Your body carries the spore that brought you here. If enough of your blood is spilled, you could contaminate the entire world. You'd also probably destroy me. I couldn't stop the spore from collapsing millions of people to light. *Millions* of collapsed lives inertially trained on me! Their light would smother me. I gag just thinking about it."

"This whole thing sounds unwise to me. I could cut myself shaving and infect a continent."

"Don't shave. Nicks are dangerous. The lynk is designed to control only trace quantities of spore, like the cubic centimeter of blood normally lost in a bowel movement. Any more is dangerous. But you can be careful. And remember, you are adamized. Your hemmorrhoids are gone, the capillaries in your nose are stronger, and the occlusion of your teeth is so clean you'll never bite yourself again."

"That's not enough. It's too risky."

"I have no other foreseeable chance of surviving my sickness," the eld skyle admitted in a woeful tone. "I need this inclusion. And you're my only way to get it. You must help me, Carl."

"And expose the earth to maneating zōtl and your deadly spore? No way."

"You'll be armored, and the armor will be fitted with a device that will activate only if you are mortally wounded. Then, in less than a millionth of a second, you will be collapsed to a point smaller than an electron."

"And that's supposed to make me feel okay about going back?" A clutchful of emotion squeezed Carl, and he felt anguish, not for himself but for everyone else he would be damning if he failed. "Won't you just help me with Evoë and leave the earth alone?"

"Even if I were indifferent to my survival, I can't help you by myself. The Rimstalkers have the weapons that you need to confront the zōtl, and they won't give them to you. They are repaying me an old debt, and it is a rare favor from them. I would not waste it in a mere act of altruism. If you won't help me, I can't help you. I'm sorry, Carl."

Through a spell of sinewed time, Carl struggled with the thought of endangering the earth, until memories of Evoë in the claret light of Midworld swarmed him. And—with trepidation clanging in him—he decided to gamble the entire human race against Chaos for the love of a woman.

A shriek, a scream, a shout of submission, a music of horror was his reply. But it was muffled in the silken chords of his suspended body, and what he mentally focalized was: "How do I handle the zōtl?"

"Your armor is built around a light lance," the eld skyle responded with an alacrity spurred by gratitude. "The lance conducts every range of light, from visible luminescence in all colors through bolts of lightning to gravity waves. And its use will be inbuilt into your brain. You'll be able to fly and maneuver more deftly than needlecraft. And the lance also carries inertial pulses that can pierce and destroy anything. The zōtl have no defense against it."

"How will I get the manure?" Carl asked, the clockwork of his fate clicking with logic. "I'll need money to buy and warehouse the stuff."

"You'll have unlimited funds. With the lynk and the light lancer armor, you will receive a third and final artifact, an interfacing magnetic plate—an imp. It looks identical to a charge card, only it's pure white. Insert it into any bank computer system and you will be credited with large sums of real capital. The imp will also serve as your lynk-monitor. When something malefic of the World passes through the lynk to earth, the imp will use a tone to alert you. You must respond at once to prevent the infestation of your planet. Use your light lance to exterminate whatever comes through."

"And if the authorities catch on to me?"

"You must be discreet. The power in your hands will be a great temptation. You must resist the urge to use your powers for personal gain. That will only further endanger Evoë and the security of your planet. For the ten weeks that the lynk will be inertially converting the payload, you must try to lie low. We will be out of direct contact. You will be on your own. If you fail, there is nothing I can do to save you—or Evoë."

"I won't fail," Carl insisted, though his insides were a vortex of anxiety.

"Good. Then I have one last strand of advice for you. Forget your name. Don't use it."

"What'll I call myself?"

"Make up an unusual name. Something with wit, perhaps, but something obviously unreal, partaking of the anonymity of the archetypes. Why? If you have any dealings with your fellow humans and they believe you are fundamentally no different from them, they will try to take your power. They may succeed. After all, your weapons are just artifacts. And that would ruin the whole venture. I advise you to stay unknown, nameless or myth-named. Hide in your armor if necessary. You will be surprised how comfortable light lancer armor is."

"But what'll I tell people who ask for my name?"

"In the twentieth of a cycle that you've lived in the World, have you ever pondered your newness and why you are so unlike you used to be?"

"Often."

"You admire your hairy scalp, the sharper definition of your musculature, your keener mind. But who was that bald, podgy, unaware self you lost—and where did it go?"

The pause expected a reply. "I was converted by you. You extracted my defects and built me up again."

"I ate you, absorbed your inertia, the substance of your *place* in the cosmos. And I excreted you. Your perfection is my waste. You are toxic to me. You are made of my sludge, animated by my own inertial resonance—my pleasure—at the invigorating taste of your old self, its wholeness, its place *inside* the flow, one hundred and thirty billion years deep in the life of the universe. You are just the shade of that orgasm. The real you has been nutritively dispersed throughout the five-space range of my being. Carl is gone. And the you that will be returning to earth is not, at the core of things, human. Your inertia is unearthly. You belong to the Werld. And the Werld will be much with you. Remain aloof from the humans. Use a name that will bolster your solitude."

Carl hung mute in the staring blankness. He was nothing. He was just the urge of his senses folded within the mighty power of the eld skyle. He wasn't even human.

"A name will be provided," the eld skyle said. "It is best that you not think too deeply now. What I have told you has been imprinted in your brain and will be available as you need it. Skills will come with the weapons. All you need is within you."

"You could be a priest."

"In a moment, I will drop you through a lynk that falls the length of the Werld. It empties into the black depths of Rataros. Endure the journey and learn. Few humans, Foke, or droppings have witnessed the mystery of the Rimstalkers. Glad fortune to you, Carl."

Carl had no opportunity to wonder then why the eld skyle called him Carl after the spiel about not being Carl, though shortly the question of his identity would change the world. At that moment, however, he was mindless, jolted by an abrupt plunge.

He was no longer hanging in a blue void but falling, tumbling, flying toward a waterdrop of light. The opening irised closer, and he shot out into the silverhot mountain-shouldering spaces of the Welkyn. His throat unclenched, and the streaming air filled his lungs.

Whales of river-glistening skyles sailed past and then the choked blackness was over him again. The no-world endlessly unwound—

Midworld's violet shadow-eagled clouds flung by, and the sudden black again.

The blackness was big as a planet. Carl stopped moving. He was standing in the absolute black, breathing shallowly to hear through the darkness. Noises shadowy as music stared at him from all directions.

Sparks like fangs winced nearby, and Carl jumped. He was naked and cold with fear. The sparks vipered around him. His feet shuffled, feeling the ground and sensing a firmness without texture.

"Hello?" he said, and his voice was an astral thinness in a vast space.

An echo seesawed around him: "Lo—lo—lo . . ."

The snaky lights jagged closer, and by their illumination, Carl glimpsed garish images, torrid shapes, coal-glinting like black flames.

The fire-slinky forms edged nearer, and the air smelled baked. The animal in Carl was running, but he knew that any sudden move would be hurtfully fatal. He knew with the clarity of his imprinting that he was already seized.

The monstered dark around him were the Rim-stalkers, the alien smiths that in a blaze of blackness were forging his weapons. And the skills that went with them. His life was to be subdued to his weapons, to the patience in all *things*. That thought came through him as the air went womb-hot and the circle of nightshapes rushed inward.

Worm-gut moistness mashed Carl, and he couldn't move or breathe. A dragonish odor of burned clay shook him. The gluey gouts of writhing muscle that gripped his body pulsed like a fever, and he went into a glide.

The cindered smell of something broken stung him awake. He was blind. For one moment, he sensed the geometry of his body, gaunt and clear as a diamond, filled with transparency, the willingness of light, but held in blackness, replete. He was a thing, waiting to be filled with his own light. He was a purpose and not a will.

The blackness wrenched away, and Carl was launched into a wilderness of stars. The brute force of light assaulted his brain, and a galactic vista burst open before him.

Welts of brilliance swelled against the emptiness of space, and as his eyes adjusted he saw the welts were clouds of stars—galaxies. As fast as a lazy thought, he vaulted toward one feathery wheel of light and arced through lanes of radiance and bands of star-chipped dark.

A yellow star hurtled closer, and the motes of planets about it caught the light in glints. One glint flashed to a shard and went filmy blue as it marbled into view.

With the memory of Evoë and their life inside a sunset that never knew night, Carl opened himself to his fall. With the weight of winter in his heart, he fell to earth.

Alfred Omega

I went down to Chinatown today for some dim sum and saw a Kwan Yin temple defaced with graffiti: NO BUDDHA! KILL GOD!

So I went inside and looked around. The place was empty and cluttered with trays of spent incense and shelves of offerings to the Goddess. I sat at an offering table and wrote this poem:

NO BUDDHA only a statue, gold
paint, wood, and a visage calm as a face
in a womb—only incense smoke
unwrapping in silence, a
movement between a ghost and nothingness.

Ever try to write a story? Notice how the characters get out of hand almost at once? That's because they partake not only of our imagination but also of our will.

Regrets and expectations. That's all I am when I'm not writing. And when I do write, I am the thing the stories come through. I am less than myself and my characters more than me.

My science fiction novel, *Shards of Time*, did pretty well for a first novel. A lot of people read it. It was nominated for a Nebula Award, and I had chances to talk with large groups about my ideas. But I couldn't get them to believe. My ideas were just ideas. No one really thinks ghost holes are real. Or that a man could fall into one and appear elsewhere, anywhere, even as far away as the end of time. Perhaps I am mad. My idea for skylands is based on a flagrant interpretation of gravitational geometry. I think I answered the meteorology of the Werld correctly, if my hunch about gravity vacuoles in the cosmic black hole are reasonable. But these are trivialities. To believe that Carl has gone to this place—that is madness.

My insanity is really that I don't know if I am mad or not. Reality is an open mystery, and I've closed myself off too long with my ideas and emotions. If I have to go mad to understand what happened to Carl, I won't regret it. Ignorance is worse than madness.

> Where grief meets hope
> we are all ghosts
> of our blood, limbs of the wind, unknown
> to ourselves.

Just as lines of force end nowhere, my own connections are wider than metrics. I am not imbedded in space. I am not flowing through time. I am spacetime. And more. For spacetime is not faithful to the quantum principle. I won't expound on geometrodynamics here except to say that I belong not to spacetime but to superspace, the reality "below" the Planck distance (10^{-33}cm) that projects the manifest world we live in.

At the level of superspace, the gravitational collapse that began and will end our universe is continuing now, seething everywhere as everything. Lines of force nowhere end, so the Field is here with me. Even in the void between galaxies, virtual pairs of positive and negative electrons, mu mesons, and baryons are continually being created and annihilated. Created by what? By the Field—the pregeometry underlying spacetime. It is here, right here where you are. You are made of it. You are it. The point of departure. The metric elasticity of the vacuum energy. You are nothing becoming everything.

> KILL GOD with the dead of night
> and the wound of dawn
> becomes your wound. Lack leads
> the way in.

I rest my life on the darkness. I lay down my soul. I am nothing.

Last month, I was arrested. I hadn't paid rent or bills for three months, and one day the police came. I was inspelling when they arrived. They thought I was in a coma. So I was taken to a hospital and from there I was brought here to this narrow bed in this empty room. They say I'm crazy. I've tried to explain about inspelling and how the mind is a condensation of the Field. But my explanations do sound like madness.

I don't know yet why this has happened to me. But the knowledge is here somewhere. The knowledge is always here. Like inertia, holding us in place, keeping us whole.

I'm sure my imprisonment will end soon. I sense an ending that will clarify all beginnings. I tease the guards and staff with a cartoon personification I've begun doodling everywhere: Alfred Omega, a volt-legged imp with with powers strong as a god's.

Look, I tell them—I tell you—there are ghost holes all around us. And *inside* us! They are carrying us down the years. And as we go, anything can happen.

> Living in the world, life is home,
> death is life
> having its way with us, and pain is
> the piece of our mind we give
> back.

—excerpts from *The Decomposition Notebook*
  by Zeke Zhdarnov

Quills of stratus clouds glowed red in the purple sky, and several meteors flicked over the streetlight-trellised skyline of Ridgefield, Indiana. From the tool-shed on the knolly backland of his farm, Gareth Brewster could see across the dark lumpy hills to the town's business center. He worked there in a bank as the credit-card manager. And at the end of the day, he liked to walk out to the toolshed on the grassy hummock and look at the bright amulet of the city.

Gareth had been doing that for years now. But this one night was somehow like no other. The ambered horizon beneath the last sliver of the hatched moon mesmerized him. The wind smelled of the meadows—and something new, a thin line of acrid burning. At first, he thought that was the industry at Gary, and he fulminated mentally about writing the environmental board. . . . His thoughts stilled. The wind wasn't blowing from Gary.

The brittle stink blew louder, and Gareth turned to follow its direction. He looked up at the glassy stars—

saw another needle of meteor light—and waded through the long grass after the scent. It thickened to a vile billow near the woodshed. The door was slightly ajar, and the grass leading to it from the road was recently pressed down. He stared to see if there was a fire. Not seeing smoke or flames, he turned and jogged back across the field to his house.

His wife was in the kitchen. He waved as he passed and went straight to the garage. When he came out with a shovel and a lantern, she had the window open.

"What are you doing, honey?" she asked.

"An animal got into the toolshed," he replied. "I'll be right back."

"Leave it till morning."

"And have it topple the workbench and all my tools? No, I'd better take care of it now."

"Those tools have been sitting there for months. They can wait till morning."

Gareth ignored her and loped over the soft land to the shed. The stink was gone. No—there it was, only slimmer now. The air seemed to pulse with it when he stood before the door to the toolshed. He nudged it open with the shovel and shone the lantern in.

The workbench with its spread of tools was untouched. Gareth entered and swung the light around. In the far corner of the rectangular room, a tall black bale leaned. His eyes skittered to see what it was. Closer up, it looked like the back of a hunched-over gorilla. It shivered, and the air quaked with a charred stench.

Gareth gasped and lurched about to leave. From the raftered ceiling, a shadow scuttled. Gareth stopped to see what it was, and a writhing spider, big as his hand, dropped into the beam of his lantern. Gareth swung at it with the shovel, and it snagged the edge of the spade with its crablike legs and spurted down the length of the wood handle to his arm.

With a shout, he dropped the shovel, but too late. The thing was on him! In his terror to swat it off, he dropped the lantern. It rocked to its side and filled the room with an orange, fractured light.

Almost instantly, the spider dashed over his shoulder and onto his back. With flailing arms, Gareth tried to brush it off while he rushed to the door. Its legs scratched the back of his neck and tangled in his hair, and as he reached for it, the thorns spurring the creature's long front legs stabbed his wrists. He slammed into the doorjamb, and spun about to see the black shivering bale in the corner lean over and reveal a glistening blue slugface, frothing with a putrescent ferment of juices. The sight of it made him scream.

The spider gripping the back of his head shimmied tight against his nape, and its powerful beak jabbed him, piercing his skull with a sound like the crunch of gravel. Its probe needled into his brain, and jagged electric colors tore through Gareth with a searing agony. His body thrashed, and his brain went rubbery. He couldn't move. He couldn't yell.

But then he was moving. Through the jackhammer throb of his hurt, through the sheets of flame snapping within him, he saw himself weightlessly rising to his feet and sleepwalking toward the slugfaced thing in the corner.

Horror was a mote in the hugeness of his pain. The very grip of his skull seemed a mere bauble in an ocean of boiling. Freezing torment scalded him, and he was floating through it to the mucus-webbed fibrils of the thing. His body bent at the waist, and his face fit into the quivering maw of the slugface.

The racheting anguish of his body stropped sharper, walloping him to an excruciating pitch of dying.

An hour later, his wife went out to the toolshed to find her husband. All was dark. The air smelled doomful. She called his name several times.

"Gareth?" The toolshed shambled with noise.

"Gareth." The door lazed open.

"Gareth!" He appeared in the doorway, pop-eyed, his face shining with the chrism of his possession. The terrible hurt dawdled on his wrung features. His face went slack, and finally his lips bent like iron into an overjoyed leer.

"Gareth—are you all right?" His wife didn't dare touch him. His face looked sunburned. "What's happened to you?"

His voice was tricked with grogginess. "I stumbled and took a fall. I'm a little dazed."

"What's that on your face?" she asked, wincing against the brunt of the malodor clinging to him.

"Turpentine. I knocked over my paint bottle when I tripped. I'd better get cleaned up."

"I'll call Doc Burkard."

Gareth's pop-eyed gaze thumped with alarm. "No!"

His wife touched his shining neck fur. "Your neck is cut open, Gareth!"

"I'm all right," he assured her in his numb voice. "It's just a scratch. Believe me."

With much trepidation, his wife obeyed him. By the next morning, she was glad she had. Gareth was himself again, and the wound under his skull looked like nothing more than a welt.

Gareth went off to work as usual. All the habits were still there, intact. His laughter was warm, his handshake crisp. No one thought for a moment that he was different—except for the two others who were as different as he.

They met at lunch in a local diner. Nothing unusual was said among the two men and the woman who gathered there, but a foul stain spread in the air around them. And when they broke up after lunch, the diner smelled sour as an outhouse and customers turned away.

The fetor was under control by the next day. The zōtl had made the fine adjustments to this more acidy breed of Foke. The brain of this food was much the same as the Foke brain and an equally bounteous producer of the adrenergic pain molecules the zōtl craved. Here was a whole planet swarming with these slow-motion delicacies, and they had stumbled upon it wholly by accident. Their mission had been to ride the Rim looking for gateways out of the black hole. When they had crossed through one, they were to test the lynk technology they carried with them. No one had expected this test run to find food. They immediately set to work constructing a lynk large enough to accommodate their jumpships.

Carl Schirmer watched the zōtl from inside his light lancer armor deep in Enderby Land, Antarctica. His armor had sensed the zōtl as he entered the blue shadow of the atmosphere at the end of his flight from the Werld. It informed him that a squadron of zōtl needlecraft had lucklessly detected his timelag echo the moment the Rimstalkers propelled him into the center of the ring singularity. His drop into the superspace of the black hole etched a minute trail of doppler-shifted photons on the roiling surface of the Rim's event horizon. By ill chance, a zōtl squadron were scanning that exact region at that exact moment. They interpreted the tiny gravity hole as a natural phenomenon, one of the frequent wormhole percolations along the Rim's horizon, and they were able to ride his lynk through the gateway to the multiverse, arriving on earth shortly before he did. Only later in Galgul, when the flight records were finally examined, would the zōtl realize that the lynk was Foke-shaped. His armor detected them at once and took him south, landing him among the fields of wind-combed snow and pack ice.

Examining himself, Carl saw a body of iridescent energy, opalescing in the polar darkness. He felt invisible. No awareness of cold or warmth. Only a sense of center, a jewel-cut silence, temple-spaced inside him. From there, his armor showed him everything. He witnessed the three needlecraft that had slashed to earth before him, and he saw the bulky females dragging themselves into coverts while the needlecraft were hidden underground. In the earth's buoyant gravity, the arachnoid males easily hovered into an attic, a tree, and the rafters of a toolshed to await their new hosts.

Since the zōtl and Carl had come from the same fargone place in the cosmos, they were inertially bonded. The sensors in Carl's armor telepathically connected him to them. He was there when Gareth Brewster and two others like him were taken. He felt the lightningflash of the zōtl stab, gouging the brain, dazzling the body with another will.

He stayed in a dreamstate with that ugliness, his armor standing in the lucent darkness of Antarctica and the wraith of him nightmaring what the aliens were doing with their stolen bodies. Eventually, the zōtl were at home with their new lives, and the whale music of their thoughts settled into the steady rhythms of their work. Days had passed.

Carl felt no hunger or fatigue. His armor had liberated him from the physical dimension and sustained him in a luminosity of euphoric alertness and stupendous rest that he called no-time. He named it that because when he was in that state, what seemed moments were really days. Time was easy.

When the snow plumed around him with the

thrust of his departure, the armor made him know how long he had waited and where he was going. Armor was not an exact enough name for what enclosed him. He seemed sheathed in lightning, a slick spectral mist that covered him from head to foot. He jetted north into the sunrise, and where the light hit him he glossed like gold.

Carl's long travels on the fallpath had well prepared him for flight, and he was comfortable with the motion-bristling terrain running below him. The strangeness for him was the emptiness of the sky, the fierce circle of the sun, and the endless continuity of the geography. This wasn't the Werld anymore.

Villages and towns darted by. Forests and jag-edged cities. A coma of blue water. Islands. The bayou cities and a bullet-fast run up the Mississippi River. Some people on boats and in planes saw Carl, but they didn't know what they were seeing. He was traveling low and at a blur that most people never noticed or simply ignored.

Over Arkansas, Carl banked through the clouds and stayed out of sight. He didn't have to see where he was going. His armor knew. Minutes later, he landed in the tree haunts of the Barlow, Arkansas, city park.

His armor shut down, and he wobbled against gravity. Earth air, fragrant with pondy odors, webbed about him, and he noticed that the Rimstalkers had clothed him in Foke strider pants, something like coarse jodhpurs, and a silky red finsuit top, flouncy with vents. He looked like a Vegas act. In his right hand he even had a baton. The black-latticed gold rod was his light lance. It had the heft of a lead bar.

Carl sauntered out of the park and stopped cold at the sidewalk. The streets were filled with silent cars in styles he had never seen. How long had he been away?

He went over to the kiosk at the mouth of the park and looked at the newspaper.

WORLD UNION OKAYS TRADE RULES. The date was two years after he had vanished. A perusal of the newspaper revealed that this was quite a different earth from the one he had left. Cars were electric. Electricty itself was generated in vast arrays of solar panels in orbit about the earth and beamed to communities as microwaves. There seemed to be only one government worldwide— but that was all he could surmise at once, since the vendor was making noises and he had no money.

In Carl's sleeve pocket was the imp, the magnetic plate the eld skyle had promised would be as good as money. It was entirely blank until he tilted it toward the light; then, the name ALFRED OMEGA winked at him. The divining power in Carl tingled, and he knew that this was the name the eld skyle had chosen for him. He didn't take to it at once. It seemed silly at first, then flippant, but ultimately apt. Alpha Omega was the beginning and the end: Alfred was an Anglo-Saxon name meaning "supernaturally wise"—and he certainly had found, or been found by, a wisdom at the end of time, the omega point, that to him and to any human would seem supernatural.

Carl walked immediately to a bank and inserted the imp card in the automatic teller. The crystal display showed that he had several hundred thousand dollars at this branch. He withdrew the card and entered the bank.

The bank officer who greeted him at her desk commented favorably on his attire, asking him where he had gotten his heel-thonged sandals.

"Crafts fair," Carl told her and then quickly brought the subject back to finance. She helped him to withdraw several thousand dollars on the validity of his ID. The blank imp was sponsored by a magnetic imager that projected directly into the visual cortex of the brain whatever an individual needed to see to approve of Carl—or, rather, Alfred Omega. Carl accepted the money with fingers that felt like fog. He was beginning to glimpse the power the eld skyle had warned him to control.

The bank officer also helped him to plug into the financial trunkline and assess all his holdings at other branches and even at other banks. They never finished counting his assets. They gave up after a half billion, and with the bank president they called together several lawyers and established a regional corporate subdivision of Alfred Omega Ltd.

They appointed a president, and as the first order of business, Carl charged him to begin at once to purchase three point five tonnes of fresh pig manure. To allay suspicions and grease the wheels, everyone involved was paid handsomely on the spot, and princely salaries were meted out to the people Carl selected to work for him.

Carl didn't actually select them. Carl didn't do anything but respond to the eidetic suggestions spilling out of him. The gravity of large sums of money drew together the people needed, and he merely released those funds through his imp. It was all transacted by computer, and he signed nothing.

Once his business had been completed, Carl left the bank and returned to the park. From a maple-hung bunker hidden from the fairway of the park by a large boulder, Carl activated his light lancer armor and arrowed into the clouds above Barlow.

A moment later, the armor put him down behind the empty stadium at the University of Arkansas. The idea kindled in him to go to the School of Science and Technology, a congeries of buildings gleaming in Arkansas red marble on a nearby knoll. In the central building, he asked one of the secretaries to put his imp card in the school computer's magnetic reader to see if his scholarship funds had cleared.

The secretary politely referred him to the bursar's office. Carl smiled charmingly and held up his imp card.

"Why didn't you say you were a Union scholar?" the secretary asked incredulously, taking his card.

He shrugged, and she inserted the card in the slot of a computer console beside her. The video display crawled with data about world history and then went blank. The card popped out.

"That's weird," the secretary wondered. "I've never seen it do that before."

"And it probably never will again," Carl said, reaching over and taking the imp from her hand. "I accidentally dropped it in front of a skateboard yesterday. I'll take it back to the registrar. Bye."

Carl was barely out the door when his armor flashed on and he was boosted into the empty sky. No one had seen him. The armor had an uncanny sense about that, and Carl queased with the thought that the weapons he had been given were smarter than he was.

The light lancer armor flew him south, back to Antarctica. He came down beside the mile-high terminus of a glacier where the moraine rocks covered the ground like knives. The armor glowed more softly, and Carl slipped into no-time.

During those early days back on earth, Carl was still ringing with what the eld skyle had told him. He wasn't human anymore, and he didn't try to act as if he were. He thought idly about Evoë and the utter beauty of the Werld—a place where colors and moods existed that could never be real on earth. The snarling shapes of windcut ice and the hurtling winds in the darkness at the world's edge were more beautiful to him than the settled places he had seen on his flight.

After the open simplicity of the Foke, ironwrought human cities seemed oppressive—and after the bold glassy architecture of Rhene and the gravityfree jumpships and flyers of the zōtl, human science seemed puny.

What did grip Carl's attention was the revelation that this earth was not the earth he had come from. Finding out where he had arrived was the reason he had gone to the university. Its computer was patched into WEB, the World Educational Board, and the imp had absorbed its encyclopedic data.

At Carl's leisure in no-time, he learned about earth-two. History was skewed, but only in recent times. World War Two never happened. World War One was so terrible with air torpedoes of nerve gas and rocket-launched germ bombs that the Twenties were putrid with global plague. The world population was halved. Political boundaries collapsed. What was left of the Bolshevik Revolution and the League of Nations unified in the early Thirties. Ideology was abandoned, and medical and agricultural technology became the necessary focus of civilization. Power brokers still ran the world, but the disruption of nationalism and the emergence of a planetary identity initiated a peaceful and creative era in human history.

Earth-two was smaller in population by over a billion, but it was larger in extent. The moon had been colonized for mining and research purposes since the Fifties. Two manufacturing centers in cislunar orbit had been producing a third of the earth's steel from lunar rock since the late Sixties. And now in the Eighties, the planet was celebrating the twenty-fifth anniversary of the end of famine and the fiftieth anniversary of the World Union.

Problems were no longer political but class-based.

Robots were replacing the working class and computers the managers. The greatest problem facing the Union was how to handle the riots of the many who wanted more than the standard provisions they were allotted.

The struggle for money and power was the same as on the world Carl knew, but the context was safer. Without nuclear weapons and international boundaries, the planet was a more secure place, and Carl anguished in his brief spells out of no-time that he had poisoned the earth with zōtl.

In no time, he monitored the aliens, feeling their sinewed fusion with their hosts and hearing the clicks and whistles of their thoughts. Work on their lynk was going well. No one in the community had yet suspected the zōtl's existence, and there wasn't the slightest alarm among the residents of Ridgefield.

Most of the possessed citizens' relatives and friends were pleased with the changes they detected in their loved ones, a few were exuberant, and none thought the worse for the cordial behavior these people displayed. The zōtl had to be liked by their prey until the lynk was done.

Carl waited, dreamstrung in no-time. Question was asleep. He did not question. He did not think. The drumbeat of his life lolled him peacefully until he felt that the zōtl had completed their work.

That instant, his armor surged, and his eyes jumped open to see talons of icebergs clawing far below him. Dawn had come to the south. The horizon was ruby-rimmed with the seasonal change.

Autumn leaves the colors of firecrackers whirled through the streets of Ridgefield. Evening's pumpkin light glimmered over the town, and the streetlamps mixed hazily. Gareth Brewster was one of the last to leave the bank. He waved to another manager still at her calculator and joked about late hours with the security guard at the door.

A silvery abalone light flashed through the plate-glass windows. The lock on the revolving door snarled a spark, and the door whirled with a cold fire. The figure of a man garbed in light stepped into the bank's marble foyer.

He held up a gold rod circuited with black lines, and with a loud pop Brewster erupted into sparkling silver-blue flames. He was kicked backward by the force of the blow, and his flame-jetting body careened over the glossy floor and hit the tellers' wall with a splash of fire.

The manager, who had seen this from her desk, screamed, and the security guard crouched with fear at the appalling sight of Gareth's blackened body hived with wormy energy.

When the guard reacted, spinning about, his pistol drawn, the figure of blinding abalone light was gone.

The light lancer armor had done the killing. Carl moved with it, knowing the fire-gusting body had been zōtl-infected—possessed because of his return—but not feeling that knowledge. Nothing reached him at a feeling level. Not until after he arrived at the toolshed on the backlot of Brewster's land where the lynk was being built.

The remaining two zōtl were there with the females. One had already been sent back to Galgul through the lynk, a chrome parabola enclosing a crystal light iridescing with movement. After the female had crossed, the light went out.

An explosion shook the air, and Carl came through the wall. A side of the shed collapsed, bruising the night with the glaring hues of the lynk's frame.

A woman with gray bobbed hair and black marmo-set eyes stood before him, shaken with fear. She was zōtl, Carl knew. The other zōtl, a bald, jowled man in a T-shirt was loading a female onto the wood ramp sloping to the lynk. "Rimstalker!" the woman awed.

Carl willed himself to finish these two and be done, but the armor did not respond.

"Rimstalker, we are zōtl." The old woman stepped closer. "We are not here to fight. Don't provoke us."

While she spoke, the man edged toward the workbench at the side of the lynk. He jumped, snatched an object off the bench, and rolled toward the lynk in a blur of inhuman speed. The crystalline light jumped brightly inside the lynk.

The armor, which Carl had been urging with all his mental powers to react, moved suddenly. A flare of energy squashed the man and a second burst kicked the woman into a blazing husk.

Carl went over to the lynk and picked up the object the man had grabbed. He knew then why the armor had waited. The object was the gate device for the lynk. Only a zōtl will could activate it. Once the zōtl had opened it, the armor had slain them.

Carl approached the open lynk and pointed his light lance into it. The lance bucked like a shotgun, and the lynk hues vanished.

Carl pushed the chrome arch down, jumped into the sky, and dropped a ball of writhing electric vipers onto the toolshed. The entire hillock disappeared in a white blare of silence and reappeared an instant later inside an oceanful roar of thunder. The toolshed was gone, and a broth of silver mist swirled in the crater where it had been.

The armor shot Carl high over the avalanching thunder, and he was told what had just happened: The armor had waited for the lynk gate to be opened so that it could fire a gravity pulse into the lynk. The pulse was amplified by a tunneling effect and came out the other end as a gravitational tsunami. Half of Galgul was probably destroyed outright, and the zōtl World empire seriously crippled.

The information swept through Carl like a black undercurrent. *Evoë!* He had probably killed Evoë. But not him! It was the armor!

The despair of that thought clashed with the armor's mounting wavefront of euphoria, and a felt-before craziness, like a dream remembered only in sleep, shuddered his mind. He flew through the length of the night, until the brink of the world fell below him and the sun jolted his eyes.

Who was living him? All at once the idea of abrogating his will to the Rimstalker's armor was a horror. The zōtl were gone and the eld skyle's medicine being gathered, but his Evoë had been sacrificed. A scream banged for a way out.

Carl forced his attention into himself. He wanted to feel his own will, slight and muddling as it was. He didn't want to scream. He wouldn't break down. He just wanted some control of his own actions.

The armor obliged, and Carl, hagggard with uncertainty, flung himself toward the wall of dawn.

* * *

SCI-FI MURDERER SLAYS THREE
THREE KILLED BY LASER MONSTER

The headlines glared from where they lay on the mail carriage that clanked by Zeke Zhdarnov's room six days a week. He wasn't allowed newspapers—they fed his delusions—but Chad, the attendant, usually placed the papers on top of the mail carriage and left it where Zeke could read them through the steel mesh of the door.

Lately, Zeke had not been coming to the cage door.

He was dreamward again—inspelled, he called it. Dr. Blau said it was catatonia simplex. For Chad, big gladsome Chad, it was the prelude to Out, that wakeful, brotherly, and voluble state Zeke got into after inspelling. He came out of his trances hungry for human contact. And Chad was always happy to face into his light-year-long stare and listen to his mild, almost fatherly rantings about ghost holes, inertial waves, and infinity.

Chad was happy to indulge this lunacy because when the old man was through he was in a grateful mood and he always showed his gratitude by naming a winner in the next day's Daily. Chad never told him that he played the horses, the old man just told him the winners' names on his own. And he was always right. The winners were invariably low-paying odds, but Chad had become accustomed to the regular stipend. And he'd learned not to question Zeke—the old man babbled like a washer-cracked faucet anywhere near a question. And, of course, he never told anyone else. It would have watered his odds at the track, and no one would really have believed him anyway.

He'd seen the old man do wilder magic than horsebetting with Dr. Blau, the chief of staff, and no one was impressed. Like the time Zeke knew everything about Dr. Blau, even his family secrets from the Great War, and the chief of staff explained it away as an afflux of the collective unconscious and ordered the old man shot up with depressants.

But drugs didn't affect him. After the shots, Zeke slumped to sleep, and once the staff were gone he'd get up. When Zeke was medicated, Chad sometimes pretended to work in the rose garden, near the vine-knotted trellis from where, with the slant of the afternoon rays, he could see into Zeke's room. The old man moved about his cubicle with slow-motion ecstasy, arms held up limply like an orangutan's, face luminous as a child's. He was talking with the cosmos.

Zeke, naturally, was not really an old man. He was thirty-six. But in the last two years every strand of his black hair had gone white, and he had grown a full beard that on his brawny frame made him look like an aged mountain peasant.

He himself no longer knew if he was mad. And he didn't care. He had tapped a creative surge within himself that endowed him with a calm self-absorption. The surge was cosmic. It waved through him with the rhythms of cloud-shadows, the spill of the wind. He couldn't predict or command it, but when the surge was on him, everything seemed possible. The buzzing chords of his body relaxed, and a soft alertness rose through him, peaked to an energetic wherewithal, and eventually eased into a quiescent clarity.

Zeke had found this rhythm before he had been brought to the asylum. He had found it the rain-pattered night he had decided not to question his feelings but to search for Carl wherever the search led.

The conclusions his reasoned search had found were so bizarre that no one thought them real. And when he took them seriously, his former friends and colleagues avoided him. He didn't blame them. He no longer belonged in society. He was a cosmic man now. What else could he be after pondering Carl Schirmer's fate and deciding he had actually become light?

In the journal he kept to monitor the evolution of his thoughts, a journal he had named *The Decomposition Notebook* to signify Carl's transformation though it just as aptly applied to himself, he wrote: "Ignorance is worse than madness." And soon after that his inspelling went deeper and he woke up in the asylum.

During one of his first inspells, a year before, lying on his back among his scattered books and papers, seeing the blank ceiling as a vast cloud of atoms, he felt a fantasy with the musculature of a conviction. He imagined that Carl's body of photons had not only collapsed through a ghost hole but had expanded through that same hole into another universe. And not an entirely random universe. Whatever had collapsed Carl had used its own inertia to guide Carl's light through the ghost hole to itself.

This hypermetric entity Zeke called an urg, because it sounded like erg, which was the quality that this thing had turned Carl's 150-pound mass into. $E = mc^2$, eh? Then, 69-kilo Carl became 61.2 million billion billion ergs. Enough energy to vaporize Manhattan if he hadn't collapsed into the urg.

And for what purpose? Zeke felt that there could be only one purpose for a complexly organized poly-dimensional being like an urg to snatch a scrawny, bald bartender. Carl was food.

Food to a metaspatial being was bound to be something like and quite unlike food to a human. Something like, in that nutrition would be extracted from the process. But what would an nth-dimensional being's nutritional needs be?

Zeke figured an urg needed more than energy, because what people defined as food energy was not photons themselves but the timebound process of releasing photons. And a hungry urg, with the resources to reach outside of its own time and implode a man to light, could certainly satisfy its energic needs locally.

Eventually, Zeke reasoned it was Carl's inertia, the sumful potency of his wee mass within the cosmic mass of the universe, that the urg wanted. Inertia, as light, was timefree and could be transported through ghost holes to the urg's hypermetric locus where no human mind could reason its digestion.

One grand consequence of this trance-found theory

was that Carl, who had inertia but was not as a mind any particular inertia, would survive. Zeke's hyperbolic mentations assured him that it was unlikely that Carl had been harmed at all. As Carl's inertia was extracted, the alien's equivalent inertia was excreted—and because the basic conservation laws of the universe insisted on equivalency, the alien's inertia was excreted as another, identical Carl—identical but for his inertia.

Insights like that inspired Zeke's science fiction novel *Shards of Time*. And the writing of the book inspired more inspelling and more insights. The syndrome was devastating to Zeke's life in society, since he spent most of his time communing inwardly in states of mind that looked to others like coma.

But he didn't care. He was happy only when he was inspelling, which, now that he had arrived at the asylum, was almost continually.

Chad left the newspapers near Zeke's mesh door, and he was surprised when he came back to see the old man reading them.

"So you're Out," Chad chirped. "What galactic insights do you have for me today, Zeke?"

"Hmm." Zeke was leaning against his gate, reading what he could see of both papers simultaneously. "Have you read the lead story?"

"The raygun killer?" Chad asked with a chuckle. "Yeah, that is wild. Seven witnesses and a video clip from the murder in the bank. Check out those photos." Chad opened the folded newspapers and revealed the front-page photographs of a human-shaped glare, a security guard, and a man in a three-piece suit. In one of the shots, the bank manager was furry with tufts of light, his horrified face twisting with the force of a blow while the man-shaped glare pointed at him with a wand.

When Chad looked at Zeke for his response, the

old man wasn't looking at the paper anymore. His ducal face was staring through the rose trellis and into some subtle reality. "I think it's time I gave you a big winner," he said in a voice iffy as fog. He was inspelling, touching his will to the torrent of power sluicing through his deepest cells—and the sparks flew in his mental eye, flaring off his willful image of a big purse at a racetrack, until the name of the track, the horse, the jockey, and the race sparkled their brief instants in his mind. "Put it all on Blue Karma in the second race at Aqueduct tomorrow. Hidalgo will be riding. Got that?"

"Yeah, Zeke," Chad answered in a quiet tone. "But why're you giving me a big winner? I mean, I'm happy with a small purse, long as it's regular."

"You guessed, right, Chad," Zeke responded, his slim, black eyes focusing again. "Our game won't be regular anymore. In fact, this is your last chance for a sure win. I'll be leaving here pretty soon."

"Where're you going?" Chad asked anxiously.

"I don't know, yet. But I'll be gone before the week's out."

"How can you say that?"

"You see that newspaper?" Zeke nudged his jaw toward the splayed photos of the bank murder. "That man is on his way here to take me out. That, my friend, is Alfred Omega."

"Your cartoon character?" Chad was incredulous. "Man, you've amazed me too many times for me to disagree with you. But if you call this one right, you ain't human."

"Oh, I'm human, all right. And so is he," he answered, looking at the news photos of the raygun killer. "But I don't think those three he put away were. I figure they must have been spider people or this wouldn't have happened."

"Spider people?" Chad folded up the newspapers.

"You mean, like in your novel? Spider people from Timesend?"

"Uh-huh."

"You really think everything you've written is true."

"Not everything, Chad. Just *Shards of Time*. I didn't actually write it. It was written through me by the inspelling. Somehow I'm connected with another world—I think inertially, but not in the physical sense that we usually mean when we use the word inertia."

"Clam it, Zeke—here comes the doc."

A frail, cleanshaven, elderly man with green eyes and a woeful expression entered the rose garden. "Ah, Z   I'm glad to see you commiserating again."

"I'm glad you're glad, Dr. Blau," Zeke said. "What brings you to the zoo today?"

"My usual social call." He unlocked the cage door and opened it. "Routine—unless you've had some kind of insight into your condition. Is that so?"

"You mean have I abandoned my insights?"

"Your delusions, Zeke," Dr. Blau corrected, stapping the cuff of a sphygmomanometer onto Zeke's left arm.

Dr. Blau was baffled by Zeke. The patient in no way displayed the classic symptoms of the cyclothymic schizophrenic that the medical review panel had labeled him; that is, he wasn't disassociative in his lines of thought or extreme in his emotions, and he displayed no fixated neuroses except his delusion that his fiction was real. His catatonic episodes, the "admitting symptom" that had earned him his cubicle in the asylum, were profiled by singular EEG readings, topsy-turvy with theta waves at exotic intervals. Physically, his patient was sound, virtually a model of physical health. And that, too, was a problem, for Zeke barely ate enough to keep a man half his size alive. Dr. Blau had agreed to hold off forced feedings and intravenous supplements for as long as Zeke's body weight and blood chemistry remained stable. And that, now, had been the full eight months that he had been here. Initially, there had been some instabilities when they weaned him from alcohol, but after the first six weeks his metabolism leveled, and he seemed to be drawing sustenance from a current of power he called the Field.

Chad had strolled off with the mail carriage, and Dr. Blau let him go, though he had some questions for him about the newspaper they were discussing that he knew Zeke would not answer. Like: "Why did the news interest you today? I notice you hardly pay any mind to current events."

Zeke watched Dr. Blau remove the arm cuff and then place the stethoscope to his heart. Zeke's face was benign and seemed to have all the layers of light of a diamond.

"Are you getting enough sun, Zeke?"

"Now that the solar maximum is passed, I may spend more time lolling in the sun. We'll see." Zeke smiled and buttoned his shirt. "How'm I doing?"

"You have the blood pressure and heart strength of a teenager," Dr. Blau responded and led Zeke by the hand out of his cubicle. The sunlight bounded off Dr. Blau's white coat, and Zeke squinted to look at him. "You eat so little," Dr. Blau said. "How do you manage to thrive?"

"How do you grow your hair?" Zeke walked into the shade of the rose arbor. "The body does it. I don't think about it."

"But I need more than four hundred and fifty calories a day to keep growing my hair. Do you have any thoughts on why you don't?"

"In fact, I have," Zeke said, smelling a rose. "But I don't feel like telling you."

"Tell me anyway."

"Why should I?"

"Because I want to know you."

"You've had eight months to study me. You know what I would say."

Dr. Blau nodded, put a wingtipped oxford on the edge of a stone bench, and leaned his arm on his knee ruminatively. "Yes, I suppose I do." He leveled his most earnestly friendly stare on Zeke. "You still believe the—'Field' sustains you?"

"Call it the earth's biomagnetic field, if you prefer that nomenclature. But that, too, is a misnomer. The Field interpenetrates all spacetime. Here in the solar biopause we call it life. But when you're aware of the Field, you see that *everything* is living—rocks, atoms, even the vacuum."

"I see." Dr. Blau stood upright and jammed his hands into his pockets. "But why can you utilize this Field and I can't?"

"You could if you wanted. Look, I've told you all this before. The Field is there. We wouldn't be standing here talking about it unless it was real. But if you want to be conscious of it, you have to empty your head to make enough room for the experience. It's big, Doc. And without neurotransmitters like LSD to help turn off the inhibitors, the brain stays locked in its chemical habits. The mind is so much a part of the Field, it doesn't normally sense it."

"Go on."

"That's all I'll be telling you about the Field, Doc."

Dr. Blau shrugged. He signed to two beefy white-smocked guards that had been watching their conversation from the other side of the rose garden, and they approached to escort Zeke back to his cubicle. "I'm sure in a few days you'll be happy for the company," Dr. Blau said, turning to go. "We can talk then."

"I won't be here."

Dr. Blau stopped. "Oh, really?"

Zeke walked back into his room and gently closed the mesh gate after him. "Sometime in the next few days, my dear doctor, Alfred Omega will be coming for me."

"In the flesh?" Dr. Blau asked with raised eyebrows.

"Decidedly."

Dr. Blau's gray, wirestrand eyebrows lowered slowly as he mulled this over. "I'll be looking forward to meeting him at last," he said with his usual spry humor, though concern clouded him. This was the first time that his patient had expressed a deadline for his delusion. The inevitable disappointment would be a blow that could finally collapse the whole delusional system. Excitement competed with anxiety in the psychiatrist, for a collapse could be the turning point of a cure.

Dr. Blau smiled his sad, open smile and patted the mesh gate. "When Alfred Omega gets here, we'll all have a good chat."

* * *

The dark hills of the Ozarks bowed below Carl Schirmer like the bent backs of migrant workers. The sun was high, and his armor flashed bluegold as it guided him down the sky to Barlow, Arkansas. His heart was heavy as metal, and when he alighted on a rooftop in the downtown district, he sat on the edge of a skylight and wept.

Evoë was probably dead—killed by the vindictive strategy of his armor. *His* armor? He had not planned to fire a gravity wave into the zōtl lynk, nor had he intended to kill human beings even if they were possessed by zōtl. He had trusted the light lancer armor, and it had used him for its grim purposes.

Rimstalker strategy, he thought, remembering chillfully the black devil-flames of Rataros. His armor was the master—and he was the weapon.

His tears drained his grief and left him dulled. He

looked closely at the lance in his right hand. The gold metal returned a bellied reflection hatched with the black branchings of circuit lines. His face looked belligerent and stronger than he imagined himself.

At the muzzle end of the lance, an amber lens grinned a rainbow. Opposite that, at the hilt, a black rectangle pulled off in his strong grip. It was his lynk. It looked nothing like the cumbersome metal arch the zōtl had built in Ridgefield. This was just a black square he could hide in his hand, yet the inspiriting of knowledge that had come with the armor assured him that this dense, apparently inert object could transport tons of earth mass to the far end of time.

Holding the lynk, Carl's purpose flushed stronger in him. He snapped the lynk back onto the lance's hilt and walked off the roof through a firedoor and down the stairs to the street. At a nearby clothier's, he used some of his cash to purchase underwear, an expensive gray suit, tan shoes, a silk shirt and tie, and gray aviator sunglasses.

He neatly folded his finsuit top, strider pants, and sandals into a leather and wood attaché case. He also bought a black umbrella and in the secrecy of the dressing room fitted his lance into it, using gentle welding bursts to secure it to the umbrella's metal ribs.

Then he used a pay phone first to call the bank he had hired to handle his affairs and then to order a limousine from a local taxi service. While waiting for his car, he had lunch at the best restaurant he could find in the small town.

Carl had no real appetite. In fact, the armor, which was a unit small as a dime and impacted at the base of his skull and which projected the iridescent field of force around him when he commanded it, also sustained his biologic processes. Food was unnecessary as long as he activated his armor regularly. But the taste and texture of the meal comforted him with the animal recognition of eating, and he ate a large meal while he pondered his situation.

He resolved, between a course of split-pea soup and broiled trout, to do what he had been sent to accomplish, but to do it with as little reliance on his armor as possible. The musical program in the background faded, and a news bulletin announced the bizarre raygun deaths of three people in Ridgefield, Indiana, earlier that day.

Carl's interest in food faded in midbite, and he paid his bill and went outside to wait for his limo. The long black car pulled up to the restaurant ten minutes later, and he had the driver take him to the address that the bank had given him.

The ride cruised out of town, wound through the surrounding braes and hills, and eventually hissed up a newly gra⸱⸱ ⸱ed road to a long warehouse luminous with fresh ⸱⸱⸱nt. A chocolate-brown Mercedes was already parked in the lot in front of the warehouse's giant sliding doors. He dismissed his driver with two hundred-dollar bills and walked over to the warehouse.

Silverhaired Mr. Powells, the man Carl had hired to oversee his enterprise, was inside the air-cooled, dimly lit building with two of his assistants, examining the three huge mounds of pig manure heaped on the concrete floor. The stink kicked like a mule.

"Mr. Omega," Mr. Powells acknowledged Carl, offering his hand and a generous smile.

"Al, please." Carl shook his hand and nodded to the others. They met his stare deferentially, obviously surprised by his elegant and conservative appearance, having expected to see him again in his Foke attire. "Three point five tonnes?"

"Accurate to within a few pounds on the heavy

side, Al," Mr. Powells assured him. "It's raw, untreated pig manure. The largest pile in the county."

"Good." Carl motioned everyone outside. "Let's get some breathable air."

He walked to the Mercedes and faced Powells there. "You have the papers?"

Mr. Powells handed him the contract the bank had drawn up to his specification, and Carl examined it. The papers simply bound Powells and the others to secrecy in return for which they would receive substantial sums each month. After he signed it, Carl accepted the warehouse keys.

"Would you like me to arrange for a distributor?" Mr. Powells asked. "I assume all this crap is going to be processed into fertilizer."

"No—I mean, yes—but I'll take care of that," Carl answered.

"You'd better do it fast," one of the assistants said. "You'll want to recycle that stuff before it really festers. Even in this cool weather it won't be long before it gets very ugly."

Carl just smiled. He waved as they left. Once they had pulled out of sight, he turned on his armor and went back into the warehouse.

He waded into the dung, using his lance to clear his way. As near to the center as he could estimate, he placed the small, rectangular lynk. Nothing happened, but he knew in his special way that the lynk had already begun converting the inertia of the tonnage.

He locked up the warehouse and launched himself into the sky. The armor urged him southward toward the polar wastes, but his will forced against those inner promptings, bending the impulse of his flight, and he flew west toward a new freedom.

Zeke sat facing the rose garden through the cross-hatch of the gate that confined him to his small room. He stroked his lion-grained beard, and his black eyes were empty as an open grave.

Where was Alfred Omega?

Dr. Blau's green stare silently asked him that at every encounter, in a mocking way that hoped to break his "insanity."

And Chad, who had won big enough at Aqueduct to quit his job, still came by every week to see how he was doing and to ask with his mundane stories his unspoken query: Where was Alfred Omega?

Thoughts like brambles tangled Zeke's emotions with hurt and doubt. Maybe he was wrong—wrong about everything. Maybe nothing he had found in his surges was right. Maybe the mirror that never forgot Carl's last image was faithful to a different meaning than the one the science of his imagination had revealed.

He was trapped, deep in the labyrinth of events that were heavy with madness. But the events *were* real: Carl had become pure light. The surges from far in his solitude *had* provided clews of ideas that had led him on—and on—but not yet out of the labyrinth.

Shaking with doubt, fearful of his own suffering, he had to admit he was wrong about Alfred Omega. Why had he ever thought Carl would come back? The thought was simply imaginary, something he had dreamed up after his novel and then taken seriously because the subtle thread of his extrapolations had led him that way through the labyrinth. And now he realized the thread had woven a trap. He'd made a fool of himself. Worse—he'd convinced everyone he *was* mad.

He quaked for several more minutes, then shrugged off his self-pity. So he had guessed wrong about Alfred Omega. He wasn't Christ. He was just a scientist. He didn't do miracles. They did him. The Field was real.

above the back door. He tossed several more gravel stones before the window swung open and the gray sleep-tousled head of Caitlin Sweeney poked out.

"Get away from here, you!" she called down and waved her hand at him like a brown sock. "This house is still mine, and I won't have you driving me out until my proper time is up."

"Your time isn't up yet, Caitlin Sweeney," Carl called back. "Come down here and let me in."

Caitlin leaned farther out the window and stared down at him. "Who are you?" she asked, almost in a growl.

"Don't you recognize me, Caity? Has my voice changed, too?"

"You sound like—" she began, then looked more closely. "You couldn't be."

"Take another look," Carl said, removing his sunglasses. "Caity, it's me, Carl."

Caitlin's scream knotted in her throat, and her aghast expression collapsed to a wondering stare. "Carl?"

She rubbed her whole face and looked intently at him. "Carl—can this be? Jesus—"

"It *is* me, Caity," Carl said. "Come on—let me in."

"Sweet, sweet Jesus," she mumbled and disappeared. Moments later the back door flung open and she stood time-bent in the doorway, staring at him in pale disbelief.

"I've got more hair and muscle," Carl admitted. "And my face is a little stronger-looking, I think. But it's me. Remember that morning I spilled hot coffee in my lap while I was counting the strands on my head, and you said I had to work on my image? Hah! Remember?"

"It *is* you!" Caitlin screamed and rushed into his arms. She pulled back enough for her rheumy eyes to study the small details of his face. This pugnacious, blond face *was* Carl's, slimmed down and tautened. And finally recognizing him, she grabbed his thick shoulders and dropped her whole weight into his embrace. "Carl! I must be dead. I can't believe you are really here. You're more solid and real than ever."

"I have a lot to tell you," he said, unprying her lamprey hold. "Let's go inside. I have to tell all this to someone."

Caitlin immediately called Sheelagh, who was now living in the dorms at CCNY. While they waited for her, Caitlin listened, and Carl lied. He told her about his riskful adventures gambling his small savings against stock index futures and then reinvesting in a dangerous but high-yield emerald-mining cartel in Bolivia.

She bought the whole story, especially after Carl made a few phone calls and arranged to buy back the Blue Apple from the bank that was foreclosing on it.

The startling change in his physical appearance he accounted for as cosmetic surgery and honest labor in a weight lifters' camp.

Carl had been sorely tempted to tell the old woman the truth, but the subtle energy sluicing into him from his umbrella dissuaded him. And more than that: After the initial excitement wore off, Caitlin became remote. Much more than Carl's appearance had changed. He smelled different. The tailoring by the eld skyle of his alpha androstenol did not appeal to Caitlin. Though she did not know why, she was uneasy about Carl, and only his generosity with his stupendous wealth kept her from saying so.

The sight of the Blue Apple's interior, where he had worked so hard and where his old dreams had thrived, charged him with a brilliant euphoria. This had been the center of the universe for him, and now, with all the bottles, chairs, and tables removed, it was the husk of his former life—and the power in him gleamed to be here and yet so very, very far away from all that this had been.

Everything looked smaller and cheaper to him now, including Sheelagh. She entered the Blue Apple in a fleecy sweater, tight jeans, and boots. While her mother relayed Carl's storyful lie, Sheelagh walked her amazement around Carl. "It really is you, isn't it?" she said several times, her eyes threaded with a wondering light. "We thought you died in your apartment fire."

"I heard about that fire," Carl said, looking at Sheelagh's blond-downed features, slender and attractive, yet petulant, shallow with the youth of her life. And he wondered how he could have loved this woman so madly. She had none of the clarified power that auraed Evoë, none of the sexual poise that haunted his memories of his woman one hundred and thirty billion years away.

"Yeah," Carl continued, "I even heard that I 'died' in that fire. But the delicate deal I was muscling through in La Paz didn't allow me to acknowledge my real identity. I had to let it go. And now that the deal's gone through, I'm back. I really want to make up for the anxiety I've caused you girls. We are going to celebrate."

"Buying back the Apple was a good start," Caitlin said, hugging him again but holding her breath.

"That's just the beginning, friends." Carl felt expansive staring into these two well-known faces, and he made no effort to disguise his shining feeling. "Tomorrow, we're going to buy you a couple of condos uptown and a car or two if you want. Clothes. Servants. Whatever you want."

The two women stared at him with baffled excitement, hardly believing this was real.

Sheelagh brushed her honey-toned hair back from her face, as though she needed more air to keep from fainting. "This is so unreal." She touched the strong cast of his face. "You really have changed. I never would have thought it was possible." She put her hands inside the cool gray silk of his jacket and hugged him with a fervor she had never used with him before. The lavender fragrance clouding about him excited her as much as the new, rough cut of his features. "I'm so glad you're back, Carl. No one is going to believe this."

"Let's hope not," Carl said, easing her away from him. "I want to keep as low a profile as possible. I've ~ade a lot of money, and I want to share it with you, but i've also made a lot of enemies, and I need to stay out of sight."

"Nobody makes real money without making enemies," Caitlin said, her filmy eyes narrowing to better study him. "How much danger is there for us?"

The question was an honest one that rang alarms in the mental spaces of his armor. Theoretically, zōtl, or any other Werld creature, could appear in the immediate vicinity of his armor at any time. So far, only airborne bacteria had drifted through the lynk corridor that perpetually connected him with the Werld. Following the cues of his armor, he had occasionally purged the air about himself with ultraviolet light intense enough to kill the microorganisms. But it was unwise for him to spend too much time around anyone.

"The danger is mine, not yours," he lied to Caitlin, and she looked as though she knew damn well he was lying.

"Mom, please," Sheelagh said, taking Carl's arm. "This is Carl. He's come back to help us."

Caitlin said nothing more critical that day. He was indeed Carl Schirmer; she could see that now that she had been watching him. And he did have money. Lots of it. He took them uptown to the fancy boutiques on the East Side and spent thousands on clothes for the two of them. They ate at several swank restaurants, sampling the specialities of each place and getting wildly drunk.

Carl was happy, and his disguise faltered only once. At one of the cafés a tune came over the radio that brittled the laughter in his mouth and turned his eyes to December roads. The music was a synthesized pop version of the song he had composed for Evoë. Sheelagh took his hand when she saw him distancing away, and he snapped out of his spell.

Later that day, he installed his friends in a two-floor condominium in a luxury tower on Sutton Place. The cost was phenomenal, setting up an opulent arrangement literally on the spot, but Carl seemed not one whit drained. Caitlin's anxiety slackened, especially since now her drunken fits did not have to be melancholy. Her daughter's future had instantly gone from bleak to posh, and that more than anything eased her. If only Carl didn't smell so strange.

At night, exhausted from their busy day, Carl, Sheelagh, and Caitlin were sitting in the penthouse sprawl of the two-story apartment, watching the sprinkle of lights on the East River. They were sipping fine Irish whiskey, and Caitlin's eyes had cleared to a shining glow. "What I don't understand, Carl, is the mirror."

"What mirror?" The whiskey had made him feel limber, and the company of his two friends over the last couple of days had unshackled him from his concerns about Evoë and the zōtl. He had to wait out the two months before he could leave, and this was a lot more comfortable than a polar aerie.

"Zeke, the friend of yours who found your burned-out apartment, also found an image of you in the bathroom mirror," Caitlin said.

"He used a computer to make it clearer," Sheelagh added, "and it looks like you—that is, like you used to look."

"Zeke." The sound of his old friend's name felt unfamiliar in his mouth. What had the eld skyle said about Zeke? Carl couldn't recall. "What is the image?"

"It's a picture of you," Sheelagh said. "Somehow the fire captured it."

"But you say you were in Bolivia," Caitlin put in, her voice dark with doubt. "I don't see how. You worked in the Blue Apple that night."

They waited for Carl to answer, but he had sunk backward into himself, remembering that night a soul ago. He had been stepping out of the shower when he caught fire. His last memory of earth-one came back— the black kicking him into an orgasmic blackout. The ice rattled in his drink.

"What really happened that night?" Caitlin wanted to know. "The police never figured it out."

"I couldn't possibly tell you about that night," he replied softly. "The fire . . ." He stalled.

"The bathroom was a burned-out hole," the old lady said. "Not even the fire department could make sense of it."

"It's something I can't explain now." Carl stared up at the ceiling, fighting the impulse to tell them everything. The armor's inspiriting reminded him of the three that had died in Ridgefield, and the urge to explain himself dissipated. "The night was a strange one. It began a new life for me. You're my past. My dear and treasured past. I wanted to share the bounty of my fortune with you before I burdened you with the pain of it all."

"That sounds understandable to me," Sheelagh said.

"It sounds satanic to me," Caitlin flared. "Look— I've talked with the police and the fire officials. They're baffled. I've seen the mirror-held image of you. And it *is* you. Or it was." She sipped her drink. "Zeke, at first, thought you had combusted by yourself. Then he started getting these ideas about ghost holes. Either way, he says that for part of a second, your bathroom was hotter than the skin of the sun. That's supernatural."

"Mom." Sheelagh glared at her mother.

"Don't look at me like that," she said to her daughter; then to Carl: "An unexplainable fire, a locked mirror, a long absence, and then you return with fabulous wealth and the looks to rival Dorian Gray. Carl, tell us the truth. Have you made some kind of satanic pact?"

"Mother!" Sheelagh was at the edge of her crushed-leather chair.

"There's nothing supernatural about this," Carl said, affecting an amused smile. "What's happened to me is mysterious but not occult. It'll all make sense someday when I can talk about it. But now, I want to know about Zeke. How is he?"

Caitlin's response was sharp as a whip: "He went mad."

Carl shifted in his seat, alarmed by the old woman's antagonism. The eld skyle had known Zeke had suffered. The confirmation of it burned. "Where is he?"

"At the Cornelius Psychiatric Hostel. It's an asylum on Long Island," Sheelagh told him. She reached over and put a hand on his arm. The solid muscle banding his wrist amazed her. "He's pretty bad now. But for a while, just before his breakdown, he went through a brief creative spell. Painting, plasticine models. He even wrote a novel."

"You have a copy?" he asked.

"Somewhere. It'd be easier to get one at a bookstore. I see it around. It's called *Shards of Time*. It's science fiction."

Carl uncoiled from his seat. "Want to come with me?" he asked.

"It's eleven o'clock," Sheelagh answered, getting up anyway. "All the stores are closed."

"We'll break in. Come on." He motioned for Caitlin to join them, but she just stared at him across her drink, cold with suspicion.

Carl got a copy that night by paying a ludicrous sum to a night watchman at Brentano's. He and Sheelagh went back to the Sutton Place suite. Caitlin was asleep where they had left her. Sheelagh put her to bed, and when she came back, Carl was immersed in the book, his face stony and pale. She waited around to see if he might show some interest in her, and when he didn't, she went to bed.

A rage of disbelief mounted in him the more he read. The monotonous fear that had inhabited him since Evoë had been taken away blew off in a cold blast of horror. The book he was reading was an account of his life in the World!

The names were different: The eld skyle was called an urg, skyles were skylands, the Foke were the People, zōtl were spider people, and the Werld was Timesend. It was a story in the bold, often bloated style of science fiction:

The flyer landed on a skyland cliff among spires of fir. The pod went black.

"We'll send the flyer back," Eve's alto voice said in the darkness. "They'll only be able to trace us to here—and by the time they do we'll be long gone."

The canopy bolts hissed open, and sharp alpine air flushed in. I rolled out of the flyer, and stood up among bleached grass drooping over a whispering plunge. My eyes must have looked like raisins, for Eve sang with laughter.

At dawn, he was reading the book through for the second time, terrified by the parallel reality of its words. Only the ending was different, for it depicted Eve and Ken, the narrator, going off together blissfully into Timesend.

His eyes were red, tear-torn, and his whole body hollowed, a bubble of silence. He dropped the book and shuffled out of the apartment, needing air. He walked down Fifty-seventh Street to Central Park.

Madness is lonely, he thought at the edge of the pond, dawn spreading on the water like a tree of light. The city of his mind was frenzied with the commerce of implications and ideas. "How could Zeke have known?" was the question that enjambed "What is real, anyway?" This was earth-two. This was a place as alien as the Werld. Nothing was real. Everything was possible. Not even Evoë's song was his in this place.

Madnesses mingled in him, and he may very well have lost all perspective then and there, but the wild shout that was gathering sound in him was interrupted by the slice of a sharply pitched whistle. It was the furious sound of his mind cracking. Until he recognized what it must be: The whistle was coiling from his left breast pocket.

He reached into his chamois jacket and withdrew the imp card in a hand that went cold with realization. The sound was the warning tone, announcing that something sizable had come through his lynk to the Werld. He looked about him—but, of course, there was nothing Werldlike here: In his amazed stupor he had left his lance back at the apartment!

He sprinted across Fifty-ninth, caroming off braking cars and bounding around pedestrians. Whatever *it* was, it was back at the suite.

Sheelagh was asleep, but the sound from where Carl had dropped his gear woke her. It was not a recognizable noise. It sounded like oil sizzling in a pan, only louder and with a crackle that was almost electrical.

Sheelagh had left her door open in case Carl wanted to be with her, and she could see Caitlin asleep in her open room. She got out of bed, and the noise crisped sharper. She didn't bother putting a robe over her negligee but went directly to Carl's room.

The hot noise was definitely fuming from there. She knocked, and the weird sound went on heedlessly.

"Carl?" The door was unlocked. She nudged it open and saw nothing through the crack. She opened the door wide and only then saw what was making the racket.

The wall above Carl's empty bed was brown with the thick shape of a giant bug. The huge trilobite shimmered with the vibrations of its complex mouthparts and antennae.

Sheelagh screamed, and the thing scuttled off the wall and onto the bed. Its broad, flat body covered the whole quilt, its many thorn-spurred legs quivering with the insanity of its gnarled perceptions.

Sheelagh's scream woke Caitlin, and she popped out of her room in time to see the insectile head emerge from Carl's room. Sheelagh had backed into the living room on nightmare-vague legs and was trying to scream again, but her breath refused to work.

The monster crawled out of the bedroom, its hissing cry sirening louder.

In her desperation to get away, Sheelagh tumbled over an ottoman, and the thing hulked toward her. Caitlin mastered her terror and heaved a glass ashtray at it. The ashtray bounced off the calcareous plate of the creature's back, and it reared.

Sheelagh scrambled away from the beast and was clawing at the drapes to pull herself upright, the grotesque eyestalks of the startled beast brushing her back, when Carl banged into the apartment.

He shouldered past Caitlin and rushed into his bedroom. The next moment, he came out with a gold rod in his hand. A sight-searing bolt of lightning lashed out of the rod and struck the knot of the monster's head. The beast's death-thrash was lost in the retinal glare.

Moments later, when Sheelagh could see again, she found herself spraddled beside the stiff upended body of the thing. Firecrackers were bursting in her muscles, and her mind jumped in and out of herself in a tantrum of horror.

Carl touched her with the lance, and she calmed instantly.

"What's going on here?" she asked, her amazement expanding in her like light through the void. Her calm seemed permanent as the heavens, and she examined the dead thing without fear.

"Devil son of Lucifer!" Caitlin shouted.

Sheelagh got to her feet in time to keep her mother from clawing at Carl.

Carl swung his lance around and touched the old woman.

Caitlin's scowl unlocked, and she seemed to shrink as she settled back on her weight. "What have you done to me?" she puzzled. The flare of her animosity was like an evening color, an apricot dusk shriveling into the horizon.

"Wait for me in another room," he said to them. "I have to dispose of this thing, and I don't want you exposed to the radiation."

The two women retreated, his armor came on, and he used an inertial pulse to scatter the corpse's atoms. In a fraction of visible time, half of it vanished; the rest jumped with the impact, and the next pulse finished it. No trace remained.

Carl found Caitlin and Sheelagh in the kitchen. Sheelagh was making tea, and her mother was sitting in the breakfast nook. They regarded him charily when he entered.

The lance hummed inaudibly in his hand. "So I lied." He sat on a stool and laid his lance on the counter beside him. He told them most everything.

They listened quietly, sipping their tea, accepting what he said. When he was done twenty minutes later, their eyes were bruised with sleep. The lance was drowsing them. They went back to their beds without responding to him.

He showered, letting his anxiety drain away, dressed in a three-piece dark-blue pinstripe suit, took his lance, and left the apartment.

Carl arrived at the bucolic Cornelius Psychiatric Hostel in a limousine. The lance inside his left sleeve was cool, almost cold, against the flesh between his wrist and elbow. He put his gray aviator glasses on and adjusted his tie by the reflection from the glass partition that separated him from the driver. The car waited for him under the ivied porte cochere while he went in.

The day receptionist was just setting up in the wake of the nightshift, and she didn't look up at him.

"I'm here to see Zeke Zhdarnov."

"Visiting hours begin at ten," the husky woman said, not taking her spectacled eyes off her work. "You're two hours early."

"Perhaps this will explain," Carl said, showing her the imp card.

She glanced at it wearily. "What's a blank card supposed to explain?"

Carl's smug look evaporated. He tucked the card back in his breast pocket, tossed his eyebrows in a carefree expression, and walked past the receptionist toward the wide double doors with the wire-mesh-glass windows. If she didn't see anything on the card, he figured it was because she didn't have to.

"You can't go through there," she called after him. "Those doors are locked."

The lance tucked up his sleeve hummed. A spark snapped in the lock, and the doors swung open at his touch.

The corridor led through chromed examining chambers, which were empty, to a diagnostic room appointed with fluorescent X-ray reviewers on the wall, anatomical charts, a model of the brain, and a green chalkboard. On the board this was written in a strong, clarified hand: "First find where the darkness lies. Opposite that stands a great light."

Beyond the chalkboard were three adjacent doors. Carl sensed with certitude which of the three led toward Zeke.

"Can I help you?" A short, white-haired man with the seamed face of a shrunken apple and alert green eyes stood behind Carl. An orderly with a hulking frame accompanied him. "I am Dr. Blau, the chief of staff."

"Please, do." Carl faced him and presented the white card.

"What's this?" His wrinkled mouth turned down, puzzled. "A white card?"

Carl obviously didn't need him either, so he turned about and headed for the door that led to Zeke.

"Wait, please," Dr. Blau said, and signaled the muscled orderly to stop Carl.

Carl proceeded without hesitation, and the orderly grabbed his left arm to stop him. The shout of electricity was louder than the orderly's yelp as the invisible force about Carl heaved the man away.

Dr. Blau crouched over the fallen man and saw that he was stunned senseless but his vital functions were stable.

Carl approached the locked and bolted door that opened to the rose garden and the detention cubicles. The lock sparked open and the bolt clacked aside.

"Please, stop." Dr. Blau's voice was conciliatory. "What are you doing?"

Carl responded to the concern in the doctor's voice. "I'm looking for my friend," Carl answered. "My best friend. Zeke Zhdarnov. He's here. I know it."

"Who are you?" the doctor asked with a compressed whine.

"Me?" Carl smiled coldly. In his three-piece suit, with the stiff white collar standing up to the belligerent thrust of his jaw, he had the appearance of an underworld muscleman. "I'm just a friend of his."

Dr. Blau followed Carl in a hurried shuffle. Carl walked under the rose arbor, directly to the gate of Zeke's cubicle. "ZeeZee, are you in there?" Carl called. "Get out here, sucker. It's checkout time."

Zeke was inspelled, sitting out of sight on his cot. An ocean of light surged against him like breakers against a jetty. He had been tranced since dawn. He had woken from a nightmare of a giant trilobite devouring a screaming woman, and the fright that shocked him awake vibrated with the relief of waking into the pelagic rhythms of the Field.

For three hours he had shot through the silvered surges like a surfer. His body and its senses were merely the coast of his being, the landfall of choice, where the freedom of the light in him found will. But he was far away from that beach when Carl called to him. The sound of his childhood name rose like an immense wave and skimmed him directly to shore.

Zeke's eyes splashed open. He was hugely awake.

A generative energy coursed in the fibers of his meat, and his bones felt weightless.

"Zeebo, if you don't come out of there now," Carl spoke loudly, "I'm coming in."

Zeke unwound from his crosslegged position, stood up, and got around the corner in time to see the mesh of the steel door flash with diamond-hard light and clang off its stone-rooted hinges.

The glare hazed away, and he saw the stocky silhouette of a well-dressed man and behind him the skinny shade of Dr. Blau.

Colors swarmed into focus, and he was facing a man whose cinderblock shape, with much imagination, contained the formerly shapeless body of Carl Schirmer.

"You!" Zeke's breath jumped, though just an inch behind his startlement, he was emptiness itself. The prophecy had come true: Harsh reality was a dream. He played his part: "I had given up hope."

"I guess that's why I'm here," Carl replied. He was stunned by Zeke's appearance. The man before him was a Blake etching come to life: Job-bearded, the gelid light in his broad stare holy as health. "Let's get out of here. This place is creepy."

"No," Dr. Blau said flatly, his hair friseured by the ionization of the blast, his face pale as a fishbelly. "You can't go yet. I must speak with you. Who are you?"

"I told you," Carl said. "I'm his friend."

"I'm his friend, too," the doctor said. "You must tell me what is going on. How did you do this?" He gestured at the broken, metal-twisted hinges and the fallen gate.

"Don't you recognize him?" Zeke said in a voice like dust. "It's Alfred Omega."

Carl shot him a surprised stare. Alfred Omega had not appeared in *Shards of Time*, and Carl was uneasy about his identity being revealed. There was the ware-house in Barlow to protect.

"Let's go, ZeeZee." Carl took Zeke's arm and guided him out of the cell.

"Wait a sec." Zeke freed his arm. "I have to get something." He skipped back into the cell, and while he was gone, Dr. Blau approached Carl.

"Alfred Omega," the doctor said, his voice fugal with fear and awe. "That's the name Zeke began using in his delusions after he arrived here. Have you been in contact with him? Is this some ploy?"

Carl looked at him, bored.

"How did you blast open this gate?" The doctor looked again at the hinges, which were not blasted so much as ripped. "Who are you?"

"Doc," Carl said gently, "the world is stranger than you'll ever guess."

Zeke reappeared with a black-and-white school composition notebook under his arm. "The journal of my madness," he said with a smile bright as a joke. "It's all real, isn't it? Timesend? The urg?"

"More real than this place, buddy." Carl took his arm again. "Let's skip."

Zeke allowed himself to be led. Outside, where the morning sunlight drifted like sawdust over the garden, he saw the other patients standing at their gates, watching with mute wonder.

The diagnostic room was crowded with attendants, but no one moved to stop Carl and Zeke until they reached the examining room. There, the largest of them jumped out from behind a portable partition and locked Carl's arms in a bearhug. Two others grabbed Zeke.

A whipcrack of voltage hissed very loudly, and the bearhugger was cast backward like an unstrung mario-nette. His stupefied bulk slammed into the pursuing

Dr. Blau and knocked him onto the floor so hard he plunged into unconsciousness. The two men holding Zeke let him go.

The limousine drove them back into Manhattan. On the return trip, in the privacy of the soundproofed interior, Carl and Zeke faced each other in luminous silence for a long time.

Carl spoke first: "You've changed, ZeeZee."

"*I've* changed?" They laughed helplessly.

"How did you know?" Carl asked when he found his breath. "*Shards of Time* tells what happened to me better than I can."

"I wrote it, yeah. But only after I witnessed it. I don't really know how. I think it's some kind of inertial resonance between you and me. I was unconscious for a long time. Then my ego was killed, and I began having what I call inspelling. I think everybody has that power, but ordinary consciousness has filters that dampen the inspells to moods which most people in the blustery course of their lives never even notice. There are so many more important things going on—like getting published and tenured, like making a success of a ratty Irish pub. Madness heals that misdirection, man. We're running one path, and only the dying and the mad know it. Yeah, well, I found that out when I couldn't get anyone to believe me."

Zeke informed Carl of his image captured in the bathroom mirror. "Everyone thought it was a fake. *No one* believed his senses. And the few that did said, 'So what? A man turned to light. What can we do, think, or feel about it? It's an epiphenomenon. A once-only event. Forget it.' I couldn't buy that. I *know* you, buster. I knew you weren't a bodhisattva or a Christ—"

"Thanks."

"I just mean—what happened to you wasn't super-natural. There had to be *reasons*. And I looked for them. But I didn't find anything certain until my quest had tortured me free of any hope. Hope that I would be understood. By then I was in Cornelius, and they were hitting me with drugs. The inspelling turned to surges, heavy hallucinations. I'm still streaming, man."

"I can tell. You sound like a flashback to the Sixties. But you wrote *Shards of Time* before the shrinks got you, right?"

"Yeah. My imagination was the gateway to the truth. I know it's true now, but then it was a fantasy. A lot's happened to my awareness since that time. And your showing up is the most enormous miracle of all. But enough of my blathering—look at you! Squirm, you're a frigging bulldog now. I want to hear you tell the story."

Carl told it, and Zeke listened with a face bright as noon. His eyes bugged when Carl showed him the light lance. He handled it with the reverence of a priest. "Nothing like this was in your book," Carl said. "In your story, Eve and Ken live happily ever after in Timesend. But in my life she was taken by the zōtl. And now here I am warehousing pig manure, three people dead, and maybe even Evoë. It's crazy."

"It's crazier even than that," Zeke told him after a respectful pause.

The emotions that his retelling had churned went still in Carl. "What do you mean?"

"I mean, the urg—the eld skyle, whatever you want to call it—it didn't tell you the truth."

"About what?"

"The eld skyle told you that the Werld was inside the cosmic black hole. The final black hole. There's no such thing."

"Why would it lie?"

"It was easier," Zeke replied, smiling thinly as a

philosopher. "You see, there no end to the universe. It's forever."

"Yeah, the multiverse. I've heard of that. But our own universe is just a bubble, expanding now but eventually collapsing in on itself and maybe starting over again."

"That's the contemporary myth, and that's why the eld skyle told you that. It knew you would believe it. If you'd been a medieval European, it would have told you you'd made it to the empyrean. To a Babylonian the urg would call itself Utnapishtim and welcome you to Aralu."

"Why?"

"I told you. It's easier. The truth is too strange."

"Well—don't keep me hanging. What do you know, and how do you know it?"

"I don't *know* it, Carl. I feel it, when the surges come on me. I've seen that the universe is eternal. It's an infinite continuum, Squirm. There's no final collapse. And there's no Big Bang."

"Come off it, Zee." He looked at his friend with eyes still slippery from laughing. "What about the cosmic temperature the radio telescopes found?"

"The background radiation of space is not the relict temperature of the Big Bang. It's the heat of the Field, the inertial unity of the continuum. A black hole is not a permanent grave, either. A black hole grows. The energy it swallows is locked into it by its gargantuan gravity, right? Well, inside the almost absolute zero cold shell of its event horizon, it's the hottest object in the cosmos. Eventually, its heat gets so unbelievably intense that even gravity breaks down—and the black hole blows up! It's not an immense explosion. Nothing like a supernova. The enormous gravitational and magnetic fields muffle the blast, and the star plasma and synchrotron radiation are channeled by lines of force to both poles, where they jet into space. Over time, the material is recycled into new stars, and the process begins again."

"So where is the Werld if there is no final black hole?"

"It probably is a gravity vacuole in a colossal black hole one hundred and thirty billion years from now, nearing the time of its own explosion. But where is *now*? I'd bet this earth isn't the earth you knew before the urg caught you."

"You're right. Where I come from, there was a second world war, we've only gone to the moon twice, twenty million people starve to death each year, and we've been teetering on the brink of nuclear war for decades."

"Sounds like a real shitpot. You must be glad you got out."

"I'd be happier with Evoë, where I belong."

Zeke took Carl's arm in a grip like rage. "Take me with you when you go back!"

Carl shrugged indifference. "It's a bizarre place, ZeeZee."

"I've got to see it. I'll sit with pigshit for a couple of months and contribute my inertia to the lynk."

"There may be no way back once we get there."

"There's nothing here for me to come back to. I'm a lunatic in this world."

"Well, we're not through with this place just yet. It'll be two months before the lynk is ready to go. Caity and Sheelagh know about me. I got a little overgenerous with them, and last night one of the Werld's less docile beasts—a blood beetle—dropped through the lynk corridor to the apartment where we're staying. I was just lucky it wasn't zōtl or a gumper hog. I had to explain."

"No kidding. Do they accept what you've told them?"

"I think so. My light lance put them into a trance, and I left them sleeping."

The conversation shifted to their shared past, and Carl learned that earth-two had a St. Tim's where a muscular Zeke Zhdarnov once protected a wimpy Squirm from the abuses of the older kids. But Zee's parents hadn't died in Poland after shipping him to an aunt in Newark who died before he got to her. His parents were killed in a Hoboken house fire. And instead of Nam, ZeeZee had served three years in the World Guard and with the Corps of Workers, quelling riots in Jakarta and Singapore and harvesting rice in Laos. The parallels with earth-one were approximate but consistent.

Back at the Sutton Place apartment, they found Caitlin and Sheelagh awake in the living room before the wide windows, watching the East River slide to the sea. They both had drinks in their hands.

"I got Zeke out, girls," Carl said in a rhythm of friendly banter.

They watched him with the feral solemnity of witches. "So now it's a fugitive we have to contend with," Caitlin said darkly. "Excuse me, Zeke." Her face melted to a sisterly warmth, troubled with regret, and she went over and kissed him on the cheek, though he looked like a wild mountain man. Her face darkened again as she faced Carl. "You have to stop now, Carl, and examine your soul before you damage—or destroy— any more lives."

Carl stood squat and mute as a bureau. Sheelagh looked on from nearby, wanting to go to him, but held back by Zeke's mad presence.

"Nothing's wrong with my soul, Caity," he said. "I've lived a new life. And I'm going back to it, as soon as my work is done here. But while I'm here I wanted to see you again and share my blessings, strange as they are."

"Carl, I'm glad you've come back to us," Caitlin said, though her voice had a shiver of uncertainty in it. "And there may be hope for you, though you've got the mark of the invisibles on you. They've made you beautiful in this world. They've eaten your old face. Even so, you still have your soul. But you have to give up any thought of going back."

Carl's slack face hardened. "Caitlin, what are you saying? I have to go back."

"No, you don't." Pins of light gleamed in her hard stare. "You can renounce this whole thing while you still have a breath of life. Don't you see? You've been entranced. You're dealing with the invisibles—the faery folk! You can't take anything of theirs and hope to keep your own freedom."

"It's not that way," Carl answered with a disappointed sigh. "The eld skyle is a being like us. Zeke can tell you. It's an organism in five dimensions. It lives, thinks, and dies just as we do, only it's not human."

"And not God-minded, either," the old woman stated. "It wants a demon offering. It wants pig dung. Don't you know about the Pig?"

Carl shook his head sadly.

"The Pig is the old god of the first Druids," Caitlin went on. "It's a god-pig. Not swine but the power of swine in all of us. The Kingdom of God is within. And so is the hunger and the demonic cunning of the Pig. It is the malevolence of the old kingdoms, the beast-time, before the sacraments. The invisibles get their power from our animal selves, our oldest ancestors. You mustn't let them ally with the Pig in you."

"Caity." Carl took her hands in his and held her milky gaze with his leveled stare. "These are not spirits I'm talking about. They're not faeries. They're aliens."

"Aliens. Spirits. Faeries. What does it matter what we call them?" Her grip of his hands was cold. "You say you want to share your blessings with us, but you've only frightened us, Carl. And that beast that followed you here from hell could have killed us. What *was* that, if not a demon? It would have been better if you'd kept your money and left us alone. Look at yourself. You've got their mark on you. And unless you give up their way, you're doomed. For eternity."

Carl's eyebrows shrugged, and he let her hands go. "I guess I'm doomed, then." He sat down, dispirited. "I've brought nothing but trouble with me, all for some pig crap. Amazing. I think I'll just go back to the mountains until it's time for me to leave."

"You can't leave, Carl," Caitlin grumbled. "You'll lose your soul."

"Worse than that," Sheelagh spoke up. Her face was boisterous with emotion. "The world will lose you. We need you here. You have powers no one else does. There's so much you could accomplish."

"Listen to her, Carl," Caitlin said. "You belong here." She turned to Zeke. "What do you think, Zeke? Are we wrong?"

Zeke looked up at her from the sofa where he had plopped down. "You want the opinion of a madman?" He was still humming with the light from his last surge at Cornelius. The polychrome faces looking at him were friendly but stiff as masks.

"I don't believe you're really mad," Caitlin answered. "You're cursed with Carl. I don't know how the Lord lost you two boys. That book you wrote is a devilwork. How could you know what was happening to Carl at the end of time unless you were possessed by demonic powers?"

"What makes you think the power is demonic?" Zeke asked, his arms crossed behind his head.

"What good has it done?" Caitlin riposted. "So far you're just a freak."

"Zeke the freak." He laughed gustily. "Sheelagh and Caitlin are right, Squirm. We've been too selfish."

"Selfish?" Carl rose up in his leather chair, amazed. "You've been in an insane asylum until an hour ago."

"Because I was selfish," Zeke explained, sitting up from the sofa. His eyes buzzed, and he spoke like a machine gun: "I had incredible knowledge there—the hyperaware vantage of my surges—but I never *used* that knowledge. I wanted the knowledge to act on me—to save me. Just as you've surrendered to your armor and let it think and even act for you. We've been slaves to ourselves. We have to free the restraints of our fate and act creatively."

"What are you saying?" Sheelagh asked.

"That we should combine our resources and apply them toward a noble goal," he responded in a burning voice.

"That's comic-book philosophy, buddy," Carl interjected. "Besides, I already have my goal. I'm going back to the Werld and freeing Evoë."

"And what about us?" Sheelagh cried, the mica of tears flashing in her eyes. "You can't deprive the whole world of the wonders you've been given just for one woman."

"I'm going back," Carl said strongly. "I only looked you up to share my fortune for a time. Don't make me sorry I know you."

"Hey, look," Zeke interceded. "We all have to compromise a little to get some good out of this unexpected life. Sheelagh, Caitlin—we can't ask him to stay here with us forever. This isn't even his earth. But, Carl, while you're here, you must use the power you have to make a positive difference in the world."

"I'm not a crusader, ZeeZee." Carl was feeling harried. He had expected gratitude from his friends, not demands.

"We're not asking you to quell our riots for us," Zeke clarified. "But with your imp card, you could defuse the riots at their source. You could fill in the economic gaps that have frustrated millions."

"Yeah, and I'll probably wind up destabilizing the whole world market," Carl added.

"Don't play God, Carl," Caitlin warned. "You're right to know that no good can come of that."

"Let the scientists see your lance and your card," Sheelagh suggested. "They could learn about stuff they never thought existed."

"Nah," Zeke objected. "Too many cooks and we'll lose our soup. We have to work secretly."

"Satan works in secrecy," Caitlin admonished.

Carl got up and went to the window to stare across at the riverlit cliffs. His friends continued their debate behind his back. Their voices sloshed around him abstractly, for he was listening to them the way a Foke would, hearing English voices as boiling sounds, meaningless. Outdoors, the burning zero of the sun hung over the boxes where people lived in this world. The narrowness of those boxes and the sharp heat from the blinding pan of light in the sky choked him with strangeness.

He wanted to go home.

The Decomposition Notebook

A great battle raged against the twilight. Above a stand of palms, the bluebright strokes of tracer bullets lanced the darkness, sparking from the hulks of two hovering Hueys. A 2.5 rocket streaked from one of the helicopters and exploded in the bamboo. The red flash eeried the landscape, revealing the long body of a river.

By the fireflash, the enemy could be seen splashing through the milky water, driving a herd of water buffalo before them. The cattle bellowed with terror as the 20mm fire from the helicopters pounded into them. White phosphorus grenades glared with hurting brilliance among the advancing buffalo, and instantly the battle was cut into diamond clarity.

PFC Zeke Zhdarnov hunched deeper into the slick mud beneath the riverbank's root-tangle. The M-16 he clutched wobbled with his fear as he witnessed the immensity of the assault. Beyond the onrush of the black herd, a battalion of NVA crowded the streambed. Dozens of them were climbing the glacis, scrambling up the side of the hills, clutching their SKS carbines with bayonets fixed. Zeke turned a frantic glance to the RTO sitting above him in the root-tangle. "They're outflanking us! Let's get out of here."

But the radio operator sat unmoving.

Zeke twisted about on the mudbank and pulled himself upward by the loops of vine and root. The PRC-25 on the operator's back was smashed, and by the echolight of the phosphorus, he saw death in the man's face. From somewhere above, a familiar voice was shouting: "Get the cows!"

Two bullets sucked past Zeke's head and made the RTO's body jump with their impact.

"Medic! Medic!"—the cries arose out of the dark, and Zeke lurched over the rootweave toward them. The air was blue with bullets. Buffalo cried, and men screamed. The roar of the choppers narrowed closer.

Zeke bellycrawled into a foxhole. "RT's dead and there's a whole battalion coming down the river," he chattered to the field officer there.

"Get hold, soldier," the sergeant barked into his face, seizing Zeke's trembling shoulders. "The choppers will break the assault." He spun Zeke about. "Now get up and fire."

The rattle of a .50 machine gun sluiced from close by, but Zeke forced himself into a standing position and opened up with his M-16, firing into the blackness of the river.

At the far end of the stream, sunset illuminated the water with blood colors. Earlier that day, Zeke had helped to shovel a ton of rice from a captured VC cache into the river. Now, that rice had swollen and dammed the waterflow. In the glare of mortars, he could see the corpses of cows and soldiers bobbing in the swollen stream. Fifty black-clad figures were rushing along the bank where the command post had been.

"CP's down!" Zeke cried to the sergeant behind him. "Charlie's all over it."

"I know that, son. We're alone up here."

"Christ!" The word was brittle with the shakes from his gun. The enemy were mounting the rootweave where he had just been. In moments, he would be overrun.

Then, the sky shook. Both Hueys made a run over the bamboo, the M-79 grenade launchers in their noses blasting a hundred rounds into the mudbanks.

"Sergeant—let's go!" Zeke bawled against the thunder of the explosions.

The sergeant shook his head. "They'll chew us up in the bamboo! Stay low. Wait for the choppers."

Zeke fired a stream of bullets into the nightshadows before his rifle clip was empty. His cartridge belt was also exhausted, and he unholstered his .38 revolver.

The night curdled bright and hot, and the men looked up to see that one of the Hueys had been hit by a rocket. Its tail burst into an orange fireball, and the body of the ship careened wildly into the dark bamboo field. A wall of flame erupted, and its ghastly glow silhouetted the advancing enemy.

The second Huey pulled upward, veered away, and barreled into the night.

The sergeant cursed. "We're on our own, soldier. Scramble." He heaved out of the foxhole, and Zeke hustled right behind him. Bullets buzzed in the air. They dashed ten feet, and a volley splattered the sergeant's head into gravel.

Zeke dropped to his belly and writhed hard and fast toward the tall grass, the earth kicking up all around him. When he rolled into a cane brake, he wiped the sergeant's blood off his face. Terror made his breathing ache. He was going to die. He thought of Eleanor, the woman he had left behind in New York. Her gray eyes watched him sadly. NVA shadows flickered over the foxhole he had deserted and loomed closer.

Zeke convulsed awake. He trembled with the cold current of the nightmare and stared about the dark room for something familiar. He saw the light-flaked skyline of Manhattan, and he remembered that this was the apartment Carl had purchased on the Upper West Side. Through the open door of the bedroom, he could see the colorless hulks of furniture and the smeared light from the windows facing the Hudson.

He sat up and rubbed the tension out of his face. The war nightmares had begun after Carl had gotten him out of the asylum. Carl said they were Zeke's memories from his duty tour of Southeast Asia on war-hunted earth-one. Zeke had shaved his beard and clipped back his long white hair to the close lines of a Marine cut, hoping to ground those night terrors in the peaceful earth-two of his awake world.

Zeke's personal memories of Vietnam were serene. He, like most able-bodied world citizens, had served with the COW, the Corps of Workers that had begun upgrading global living conditions seventy years before and was going strong under World Union leadership. He had been stationed in Jakarta and had been transferred to the Mekong Delta to help with flood relief during the monsoons. He recalled a land of mosquitoes, stone lanterns, and an industrious, sylvan-thin people. They had appreciated his help, and they had shared their traditions with him. So why did he dream of spraying liquid fire on them and counting their charred bodies?

Carl had tried to explain earth-one to him—a war-world fragmented by battlelines called borders, a world of fantastic death machines and immense plunder where corporations amassed billions of dollars in profits by exploiting undeveloped nations and natural resources while in less organized regions millions of people starved to death continually. Carl had tried to explain capitalist economy and the motivations of self-interest as well as the tyrannical failure of socialist societies, but that made little sense to Zeke's earth-two mind. Economy to him and in his world was based on human interest, not personal or social interest. Capitalism and communism were both wrong. Human dignity was the only political force that made sense after the Great War, and human dignity was not possible when a few, any few, had power and authority over the many. To govern, on earth-two, meant personal sacrifice. Sacrifice and devotion were synonyms for all earth-two leaders. Those who chose to be leaders had to surrender their personal lives and serve the good, not of a faction or a race, but of the whole planet. It was an ideal that had become real after earth-two had almost extinguished itself. Earth-one would have to go the same path, Zeke realized, and until it did, it was no better than a monument to Death, a planet of atrocities.

Despite his elaborate rationalisms, the nightmares came anyway. Zeke suppressed the urge to wake Carl and talk it out with him. The man was helpful and a good friend but not the friend Zeke remembered. The urg had changed him. The restlessly jovial idealistic neurotic that was Squirm had become an insouciant watcher, waiting for his chance to return to the Werld. Zeke had been out of the Cornelius Psychiatric Hostel for five weeks now, and he still was not adjusted to the great change in his friend.

Zeke sighed and flicked on the tensor lamp on his nightstand. He opened his journal and reviewed the entries from the last few weeks. Above each entry, he had penciled in the countdown to the day Carl had taken him out of the asylum:

Five weeks before Alfred Omega

I've been pondering the chemical truth of who I am. The conspectus is this:

My madness is caused by an irreversible inhibition of the monamine oxidase (MAO) in my brain. This happened initially as a result of the inspelling that put me in the asylum seven months ago. Dr. Blau mistook my inspelling for depression. How else could he have diagnosed me? He didn't have the imagination to suspect that within the listless shell of my disconnected personality I was surging with life power, surfing the spatiotemporal wavefront of Being itself, where time breaks into Mind.

Anyway, I must have looked sunken, for the good doctor pumped me with iproniazid, an antidepressant that inhibits MAO. MAO regulates the synthesis and utilization of neurotransmitters like serotonin, and it muffles the effect of the methylated tryptamines the doctor is administering to wake me up. With my MAO knocked out, the neurotransmitters proliferate in my brain, amplifying my inner experiences—weirdly.

The surges I am experiencing are waves of these backed-up methylated tryptamines converting into the substrates for enzymes like N-methyl transferase and hydroxy-indole O-methyl transferase. Those enzymes not only stimulate the production of more methylated tryptamines, they're also psychotomimetic— they're hallucinogens!

The great space of stillness that I had found in my inspelling and from which I had written *Shards of Time* is suddenly wild with bizarre images and pulsations. During a surge, my heart hums like a grenade, ready to blast me to nothing. My blood caulks with fear, and furious thoughts of escape cross my brain like clawtracks.

That's the demon-world the Bardo masters warn about. The tryptamines have put me in touch with the tortured soul of the world, the wounded dream we call the unconscious. Actually, there is nothing *un*-about it. It should be called the metaconscious and our feeble, biology-limited awareness the unconscious. It is alive with gods and demons. The demons are psychoids, dismembered terrors and hungers hacked free of the physical world and existing solely in psychic space. They are the terrible forces that go ahead of our hope and muddle our best intents. In my life, the worst have been anger for fear's sake, lust-riddled attention, and, of course, the balloon-man with his grand, self-inflating delusions.

There, also, is God—the Archon—the metapsychic organizing power: the formless shaper of form. Its presence electrocutes me with feeling, shocking me free of rationality, time, even center.

Three weeks before Alfred Omega

I'm grateful for this time of horror. In the asylum of the State, with my bodily needs attended, my mind is free to be the horror.

Where Nature would have killed me, the State preserves me that I may know the horror and speak.

I am the Horror. The skulled mind. The weight of a scream on the tongue. The cold in the lungs as the bloodfires go out.

Two weeks before Alfred Omega

The demon psychoids and the Archon are still here, insidious and strong as they ever were, but now I recognize them in their subtlest shades. I see how they think me. I realize that my personal mind is an illusion.

The clear windows of our perceptions are actually the glimmerings from the Archon's luminous selves on the inside shell of the monad that is each of us.

I find myself sitting exactly at the center of an opaque, colorless bubble big as the universe. Reality happens around me, and I reach out and radiate my energies into the immensity, wanting to be a star.

One week before Alfred Omega

Chemical "madness" has collapsed me into the center of my monad. I'm becoming a black hole, locking into myself through the immense gravity of the metaconscious.

The illusion of individuality is almost gone. My pen is a rivering of Change, my hand is the story it writes, and I am—

One week before Alfred Omega (twelve hours later)

—the pivot of stillness before a falcon dives.

Alfred Omega

Squirm's return: The black hole has exploded!

Twenty-eight days after Alfred Omega

Withdrawal was explosive. Deprived of iproniazid and the other drugs, the Archon vanished, and the black hole of my hallucination exploded into the thin colors of skull-locked ordinary reality.

Only, reality ain't ordinary no more. Carl has come back from Timesend as Alfred Omega! I feel that I've burst into another universe where my madness is reality. What I thought I was imagining is real! These very words are quashed by the weight of their meaning, so it must read as if I'm insane. If the iproniazid and the rest of those mind chemicals hadn't been stopped, the irreality *would* have broken my mind. We need our brains to protect us from reality.

It's taken me a month to get up the nerve to write again. I know I should at least outline what's happened in the last twenty-eight days, but I'm still gonging with implications. I must understand who I am. How is it possible that I could write *Shards of Time* and describe exactly what was happening to Carl? I wasn't drugged, except by my adrenals from the anxiety of those exiled days. My writing, somehow, was telepathic—but what is telepathy? Lord knows, I can't do it at will, anymore.

I at least have some idea how I may have known things I could not have known while I was in Cornelius. Chad would be amused—

just long enough to ask me for another winner. I think my body acted something like a cross between an antenna and a hologram.

The tryptamine soaking my brain had an affinity for synaptic DNA and replaced the serotonin that usually bonds with the RNA receptor sites in the synapse. The tryptamine inserted itself in the RNA by pi-cloud stacking across the hydrogen bonds linking the two bases. The result was a charge-transfer, that is, an electron passed from the RNA to an empty energy band on the tryptamine. The swift bonding twisted the helix, and because this was happening in the electric field of my synapses, an electromagnetic signal was generated. The wave was instantly absorbed by low-energy electrons in the tryptamine, saturating their energy bands. That canceled the polarization of the base pairs, and the RNA rung rejoined, priming itself for the next charge-transfer. This oscillation broadcast its own signal in harmonic resonance with all the RNA-bonded tryptamine in all the synapses of my body, setting up a three-dimensional standing waveform inside my skull and turning my brain into a radio-cybernetic matrix. Information flooded into me from hyperdimensional realms. I experienced telepathy, conscious projection outside my body, and a spooky ability to predict events. I was turned on.

Thirty-two days after Alfred Omega

Carl has no idea who he is. He thinks he's a man. I've tried to tell him: There are no men, and there are no women. There are only fields of force.

Our bodies are starships. The Archon has spent four billion years building them. The equipment is all there, inside us, as our neurology, but the demons keep the Lord from using us. The demon psychoids of the unconscious have possessed all ten billion of the humans that have ever lived. Only a few of us have sensed the Archon. And of them, only a handful have consciously learned how to activate that power in our own bodies.

Thirty-six days after Alfred Omega

Aeschylus expressed it well when he had Prometheus say:

I caused men to no longer foresee their death.
I planted firmly in their hearts blind hopefulness.

Carl has stolen fire from the Archon. The lance makes him a god among us. Yet he remains enraptured by his memories of Evoë. Perhaps I should be thankful the archon of love has claimed him rather than the archon of power. I'm sure that's the doing of the urg. It wants Carl back. The inertial displacement between them must be immense, and every cell in Carl's body must be craving to return to the Werld. No wonder dominance of this faraway planet seems puny.

But I have no inertial homecalling to dampen my imagination or quell my will to power. Carl has seen me looking at the lance in reverie. It is not the power itself I crave.

The power is a shadow of the metaconscious.
The lance is merely a symbol of what I want.

"A balmy wind spills off the Hudson," Zeke wrote,
watching a breeze unpleat the drapes of his window and
fill the bedroom with the smell of the river. "I've
nightmared Nam again. Like everything of this tempo-
rary earth that tries for something greater, my mind
strains to understand why I am living in two different
worlds, one of peace and one of pain. The answer I
sense through my inspelling is almost unbearable: Con-
trastive thinking is an elaborate hallucination. Worse, it
is the viper I have mistaken for a rope."

Zeke turned off the light, and in the shuttered
darkness, a hypnagogic spun before him. It was a
retinal mandala, a rosemaling of torn limbs and gluti-
nous napalm-melted flesh, all blurring together in the
surfglow of his closed eyes. Before shutting his journal,
he wrote in it by feel:

"The hand is not different from what it writes
down."

Galgul was a cloud of rubble. Two black spheres
and three cracked egg shapes were the only traces of
order in an amorphous sprawl of floating debris. Blast-
twisted shards of metal and coils of black dust looped
with the fallpaths. Anything organic had been seared to
ash by the firestorm that had gulfed the exploded
structures. Inert, jagged forms hovered like a black aura
around the ruins of Galgul.

Five of the twelve clustered city-spheres had been
destroyed. Their three-kilometer-wide plasteel shells
had been shattered into junk by a gravity wave that had
bounded out of a lynk in one of the spheres. The lynk
had connected with a four-space, positively curved
stellar zone one hundred and thirty billion light-years

away. Three zōtl needlecraft had established the lynk after following a Foke-shaped gravity echo into the Rim. The conclusion was obvious. A Rimstalker had armored a Foke, had sent him to a Foke-fertile planet where the food lure to the zōtl would be irresistible, and had used the lure to attack the zōtl through their own lynk. The plan had been a cunning and devastatingly effective one.

Like two spider gods, the remaining city-spheres of Galgul hung in a web of broken metal, misty against the whorl of the Cloudriver. The broken hulks of the ruined spheres dangled like torn roots among clots of fused metal. Needlecraft sparkled among the rocksmoke and the avalanches of destroyed shapes. Camouflaged by the tumult of devastation were jumpships, black boomerangs with laser cannon, waiting in ambush for any Foke or Rimstalker aggression.

Zōtl and Rimstalkers had warred since the zōtl first arrived in the Werld, seventy-two cycles ago. Though the two species occupied the two distant poles, a Werld apart, they were both four-space creatures, and they conflicted in the tesseract range that contained the Werld. Their battles were timeflux distortions in superspace, and they fought over which species would occupy the narrow tetrad vector field that connected the Werld with the multiverse.

The Rimstalkers had dominated this gateway to infinity for the three hundred cycles of their time in the Werld before the zōtl arrived. Rimstalker technology was by far the most advanced, but zōtl four-space awareness was innately more adroit. After forty cycles of zōtl incursions into the disputed tetrad vector field, the spider people established a beachhead and, by dint of their elusive four-space awareness, were able to evade Rimstalker timeflux distortions and develop a lynk technology of their own. In another two or three cycles, they would have begun establishing a multiversal empire.

The zōtl had been taken by surprise when the Rimstalkers abandoned their superspace forays to attack Galgul with a three-space gravity wave. Within moments, the zōtl capital had been reduced to ruins. Only two city-spheres were left intact. Three were crippled, and the rest utterly demolished. And now, Foke—zōtl food—were using the rubble-clogged fallpaths to penetrate zōtl defenses and sabotage the cleanup and repair work.

This was the darkest time the zōtl had known in the Werld, and their keening warbled across the tesseract range to Rataros, where the Rimstalkers were equally shocked. They had issued the armor to Carl Schirmer as a favor to an eld skyle that had opened a channel to the tetrad vector field when the Rimstalkers were in need. Unlike the zōtl, the Rimstalkers did not rely on organic sustenance. Their nourishment came directly from the hyperphotons of the tetrad vector field, and when the zōtl began to expropriate vast swaths of the tetrad field for their own expansionist strategies, Rimstalkers starved.

Eld skyles, as five-space beings, were in a position to direct the four-space vector field to some degree. One eld skyle had been able to channel enough hyperphotons to save the lives of over a thousand Rimstalkers. In return, the Rimstalkers had armored Carl and sent him to fetch the three-space substance that the eld skyle needed for its own survival.

The Rimstalkers had never guessed that the zōtl would detect the fraction-of-a-second echo in the tetrad field, let alone follow it to its destination. That the armor had demonstrated the wit and initiative to wait for the zōtl to set up a lynk and then use the zōtl lynk to assault Galgul was not as surprising. The armor, after all, had its own artificial intelligence loyal to its creators, and it was only slightly hampered by the emotional organ the creature it occupied called a brain.

But now the Rimstalkers had a problem.

If the Rimstalkers had planned this offensive, they would have used a light lance with the power to destroy all of Galgul. Instead, the zōtl had been badly hurt but not eliminated. The Foke harassing them could not hope to overcome them. So, in a cycle or two, the zōtl would be back in the tetrad vector field and more aggressive than ever.

Some of the Rimstalkers wanted to armor more Foke and direct an assault against the remnants of Galgul. But that idea was dismissed at once in the face of the realization that the zōtl, if pressed to the wall, could use their budding lynk technology to disrupt the gravity matrix that gave the Werld its shape and collapse the entire Werld into the black hole that held them all.

The Rimstalkers understood: A three-space war against the zōtl was out of the question. They had to capitulate.

In return for a zōtl agreement to stay out of the tetrad vector field for five cycles and then only to occupy regions designated by the Rimstalkers, the Rimstalkers acknowledged that the gravity wave that had blasted Galgul was an accident, not the prelude to a three-space war. As a token of retribution, the Rimstalkers gave the zōtl a light lance and armor of their own.

The appeasement was tiny. The armor and lance were designed to implode if their interiors were tampered with, so the zōtl could learn nothing from them. Also, they were useless anywhere near Rataros, so they were no good against the Rimstalkers. The only immediate use for the armored lance was as an instrument of revenge. The Foke who had fired the gravity wave into

Galgul would be destroyed, and the Foke-fertile planet that had served as a lure would become the first conquest of the zōtl's multiversal empire.

To celebrate this new determination, the best of the suspended Foke were revived and milked.

The choice stock of Foke delicacies was located in one of the mangled spheres. There, behind fume-stained glastic panels, were several thousand human bodies asleep in no-time. The myriads of Foke were individually encapsulated and stacked upright to facilitate their gravity-pumped life support.

Among the stock was a slender woman with a quiet face and strawberry flecks in her drowsy gray eyes.

"Evoë is alive," Zeke told Carl. Zeke's eyes were blurry with drowsiness. His bear-sized frame leaned in the doorway to his bedroom, his baggy black silk pajamas scarred with sleep creases.

Carl had already shaved and dressed, though dawn was still a dark hour away. He wore a beige pair of trousers, sneakers, and a purple pullover sweater. He was sitting in the living room practicing touch control with his lance by changing channels on the TV from across the room. When he heard Zeke, his hand twitched, and the TV flew off its stand and smashed into the wall. Sparks and glass spurted, and Carl leaped up from the cushioned chair where he was slouched. "Are you sure?"

Zeke stepped over the shattered corpse of the TV and stretched out on the sofa. "I saw her in Galgul," he replied in a sleepwrung voice. "The place is a bigger mess than that TV. You really rocked it, buddy. Evoë's okay, though. I saw her in a kind of suspended animation. The zōtl are saving her for a special dinner—commemorating the conquest of the earth."

"You sure this is a real lynk-dream?" Carl asked, his head effervescent with euphoria. He wanted to believe him, but Zeke had been in a loose frame of mind since Carl had gotten him out of Cornelius. His attention had been wavery as a candleflame, and he had slept as much as he had been awake. Carl had purchased a spacious apartment on Claremont Avenue near Columbia University, and they had holed up there while Zeke suffered through the withdrawal from the chemistry set Dr. Blau had hooked into him over the past year. Today was the first day that Zeke had woken with a clear face, unscowled with confusion or pain.

The last month had been tedious for Carl. Manhattan-two was a quieter place than the New York he was used to. The hum of the electric traffic was not audible from their top-floor suite, and the serenity was driving him mad. He had used his armor to visit all the round corners of the earth while Zeke slept or Caitlin and Sheelagh were watching him. The quiescence of the cities, the geometric order of the farmlands, and the harmony of the people wherever he went spooked him. The world was closing in on utopia, and with his perpetual anxiety about Evoë and the zōtl he felt out of place and even dangerous to the world. He had already decided then if Evoë was dead he didn't want to live. It sounded stupid, but it felt right. So when Zeke told him she was alive, his blood shimmered.

The flesh of Zeke's face looked tired, yet the wakefulness in his stare was strong as black coffee. "The hallucinations are over," he announced. "The lynk-dreams have begun again—only now I know they're lynk-dreams."

"What about your nightmares?"

"I was in Nam again last night. Before Galgul. Still can't figure out how. Some kind of inertial—"

"—resonance," Carl said with him. "I know. What'd you see in Galgul?"

"Ruins. The fallpaths are so clogged with fired

debris you can walk on them. In one of the half-gutted spheres there's a stock vault, ripped open to external view. I saw tiers of bodies stacked in transparent shells. They're all alive but sleeping, waiting to be milked of their pain. Evoë was there. I recognized her at once—fauny hair, flecked eyes, and those cheeks, hollow as a cat's."

Carl looked up to the ceiling and howled, arms outflung.

"Don't get too excited," Zeke warned, when Carl was done and his face, red and polished with joy, was looking at him. "We've got some time left before we can lynk to the World."

"ZeeZee, you've just put meaning back into my life!"

Zeke watched him somberly. "Well, you'd better hear the rest of what's going on." He told him about the Rimstalkers giving the zōtl light lancer armor. "And you know it's you the spider people are going to hit with that armor."

Carl's heart became a paperweight. "Maybe we'll get out of here before they show up."

His hopefulness cowed before Zeke's stare. With his head and face shaved, Zeke had the sober demeanor of a monk. "You can't avoid them, Squirm," he said with certainty. "But you don't have to fear them. *You* didn't destroy more than half of Galgul. Your armor did. Let *it* protect you."

Carl spun about and ran both hands through his hair. That gesture usually reassured him, reminding him that he had been remade, that life was new. But now he felt closed in, and he went to the tall sliding window gazing west over the Hudson and opened it. The winter air cleared his sinuses.

The dark sky seemed empty in the direction his armor told him to look. The lynk of his lance to the

World manifested in the space of his immediate vicinity
and in a larger probability zone a mile above his head,
tilted twenty-six degrees toward the north magnetic
pole. The lynk space around him was big enough only
for human-sized transits like blood beetles, which his
lance could easily disperse as they appeared. The
jumpships and needlecraft would come in above him
where they could scatter quickly and avoid his lance
fire—until their own light lancer armor came through.
His armor did not know if it could match the zōtl
armor.

The wind turned, and the air smelled of burning
leaves. A new feeling glided in under his fear and
elation, elusive as an unwritten poem. It was awe.
"Geezus, Zeke," Carl said in a slow voice. "It's strange."

"It's always been strange," Zeke confirmed, "only
now it's gotten weird enough for you to notice." He sat
up. One hand tugged at the ghost of his white beard
before finding his chin, and he gazed at Carl, ruminative
as Moses. "Carl, I've got to talk with you."

Carl turned from his window reverie. Zeke had
never appeared as composed as this before, and the
poise in his stare drew Carl closer. "What more can you
possibly have to say?" he asked, sitting in the plush
chair beside the sofa.

"Ever hear of Egil Skaldagrimson?" Zeke asked.

"An uncle of yours?"

"He was ancient Iceland's most original poet,"
Zeke said. "But in his own day he was better known as
a ferocious manslaughterer called a *berserkir*. One day
late in his life after earning the fierce respect of his
people as a warrior, a poet, and an autocrat, he was out
for a stroll. As he passed one of his men who was
bending over, adjusting a sandal, Egil swiftly drew his
sword and—zock!—cut the man's head off. The reason

he gave for doing it is famous: 'He posed so conveniently for a blow.'"

Carl looked at his friend more closely to see if he was launching into one of his "surges." The strong face was as sensible as the Buddha's. "Okay. So what about it?"

"You're like Egil's soldier," Zeke replied. "You're picking your toes. You carry a sword, but you've lost the spirit of the sword."

"I'm not sure I follow you, old buddy," Carl confessed in a piqued tone. "If you're worried about the zōtl's surprising me, don't. My imp has a warning tone."

"The enemy I'm worried about is you. You're in some kind of trance."

"*Me?*" Carl was surprised. "This is the first day since I got here that I've seen both of *your* eyes working together."

"Sure, I've been chemically pummeled. But you've been adamized. You're supposed to be perfect."

"I'm nowhere near it."

"That's for sure. But to the urg, you're perfect. A perfect gofer. It's got you locked into its strategy, friend. You have the power, but your will has been castrated so that it won't interfere."

"Aw, cut it out, Zee." Carl sank back in the chair. "Caitlin's been trying to save my soul. Sheelagh wants to make love to me. And you think I'm a will-less zombie."

"Not a zombie, just a sleepwalker." Zeke's bushy white eyebrows lifted. "And why don't you make love to Sheelagh?"

Carl sat back as if slapped. "I'm in love, Zeebo. Remember that feeling? It's a little ways north of lust."

"Love has blinded you."

"Blinded me to what?"

"To power." Zeke's hand flashed out, and he picked

up the lance from where Carl had placed it on the coffee table. "This is power!" He waved it under Carl's nose. "When are you going to use it?"

"When I have to," Carl answered softly.

"If you don't use the power you have, the will weakens," Zeke said, returning the lance.

"Hey, keep in mind whose weak will uncanned you last month."

"I'll never forget it." Zeke smiled briefly. "But that was *last* month. What've you done since?"

"What's to do? I mean, the eld skyle didn't send me after the Golden Fleece or the Grail. We're just waiting for the lynk to convert some pig stool and then we're gone. Unless the zōtl stop us."

"Forget the zōtl." Zeke's gaze pressed into him. "If you're just waiting for the lynk, why'd you come back for me? And why'd you spill the beans to Caitlin and Sheelagh?"

"What the hell are you driving at?"

"Don't get excited." Zeke was glad to see that Carl could get excited.

"Just what are you trying to tell me? That I'm loose-lipped?"

"That you're talking in your sleep. The urg has put you in a trance, and you're not seeing things clearly. If you're loose-lipped it's because there's some of your old self left that wonders what's going on. That's why you sought out your old friends, to connect with your past and the old meaning of your life. You've lost that, and now you don't know what's up or down."

"And you do?"

"I know only one thing for sure." He leaned closer. "We're made out of light. And light is action."

"Huh?"

"Light is action." Zeke looked amazed. "Come on, Squirm, you remember quantum theory: Light is transmitted in whole units. Those units are called quanta of *action*. They're photons. Don't get me started on this subject. The point I'm trying to make is this: All creation acts. Continuously. There is no stillness. Even the void between galaxies buzzes with Field particles. Action is reality. For a human, that reality is choice. You have to act positively, and by that I mean your choices have to be creative, not historical."

"All right, already, ZeeZee. I get the idea. You think I'm lazy."

"Well, when's the last time you worked out?"

"I don't believe this."

"The urg gave you an adamized body, but how do you expect to keep it strong without using it?"

Carl was on his feet. "Riding a fallpath is a workout and a half, believe me." He strode back to the window and slammed it shut.

"The only fallpath here is down."

Carl shrugged. "My heart isn't here, Zeke. Working out's too much of a pain. I'd just as soon wait till I get home."

"That's a negative choice. Soon you'll be as flabby as you ever were. You've got to stop avoiding pain, and you've got to stop seeking your pleasure in some faraway future."

"Why?"

"It's been done to death, billions of times already. Those are the historical choices. After all that's happened to you, you can't just react. You've got to be creative."

"But why?"

"Because you've got the power, man." Zeke was standing up. As he spoke, he wended his way around the coffee table and over the gutted TV to Carl. "What's happened to you is now. It's a mandate to be original, despite the pain. You've got to use your body till it hurts. Use your brain till it's exhausted. Don't seek pleasure for its own sake. That's the game that trips up almost everybody. Let the pleasure come to you on its own—and when it comes, take it. And when it's gone, keep it a memory, not a hope. Don't look for it. Keep your focus on what you can give to others from the hurtfully alive center of yourself."

"Spare me your philosophy," Carl asked in cold exasperation.

Zeke looked down into him. "I would if there were any other way to live without regrets."

Carl ignored Zeke and turned his face toward the dark window. He couldn't take his old friend seriously, because for one thing, the man wasn't behaving at all like the ZeeZee he'd known all his life. Carl figured that was the result of the huge difference in earth-two's history: The Zeke he loved had come from a harder world where he had killed and seen friends killed in war, where death was meted out with the indifference of financial transactions—a world where the spiritual beliefs that this Zeke espoused could not be taken seriously. ZeeZee had given up all fantasies of dominance in Nam—and yet here was this look-alike ranting about power. The inconsistency left Carl with a filthy feeling, as if the memories, the life, the very flesh he was made of were not real. The eld skyle had told him that he was shaped out of sludge. And this world? Was it any different? It was made from star dung. The crap of spent galaxies. Reality *was* shit. The horror, for him, was crazy Zeke's belief that the cosmos was infinite. The Zee he knew, the world he had known, believed the universe with all its brutal ironies was doomed like the rest of them, as finite as everything smaller than itself.

The serrated aroma of fried onions and garlic accompanied the chatter of hot oil from the kitchen, where Zeke had gone to prepare a meal. Carl's ponderings smoked away, and he stepped back from the dark window. The sun's blot was behind him and below the horizon, but charred-looking clouds glowed in the east like a dragon's smoke-belch.

The pleats of cooking odors were a pale tease of memory, hinting at the pungencies and savor of the Foke meals he had known. For the thirty-seventh time in as many days, he craved a braised slamsteak and stream-chilled owlroots. His stomach growled like a rockcrusher, but he was too wrought to eat. He had to clear his head.

He told Zeke he was going out for a walk and took the stairs fifteen floors down to the street. He was flushed when he got there and satisfied. He wasn't lazy about using his body, as Zeke believed. He was afraid to use it. If he gashed himself or if he even got a nosebleed, he would probably be killed. The light lancer armor was set to implode if his spore-carrying blood was spilled.

Carl had told no one about this, and Zeke for all his apparent prescience had not found out.

He walked down the steep hill of 116th Street and entered Riverside Park. The dark blue of night was standing in the tree clumps, and the plangent fragrance of the river drifted up the terraced slopes. Why had he come back, really? Was he seeking something from his past? Of course. Yet how could he tell this Zeke about his fear of the armor? Not just the anxiety of bleeding and being collapsed smaller than an atom, but the cruelty of hosting the armor's mind inside his own— that terrified him. He had wanted to talk about it, and so he had sought out his old friends. They were all stranger than he remembered them, though. Or was it the armor mechanicking him that made them seem strange?

The moon looked like a Quaalude over the Palisades. The silvered clouds around it rhymed in his memory with the griffons of cloud that strode through the open spaces of Midworld. Carl sat at an empty park bench, and in the long light remembered Evoë. A youth went by, shouldering a radio big as an air conditioner, and the music blaring through it was her song.

Sheelagh was still asleep when Carl entered her apartment. Several weeks ago, in a schoolgirlish rush of love and gratitude, she had given him the key to her apartment on Sutton Place. Her mother had railed against her, but Sheelagh didn't care. Caitlin had her own apartment on a different floor. The old woman disapproved of fey Carl, but she didn't eschew his booty. She was fond of having her friends come by and being able to give them enormously generous gifts from the seemingly inexhaustible bank accounts Carl had set up for her.

Sheelagh was not as happy with her money. She wanted Carl. The first few weeks, she had made a fool of herself over him. She had shown up at his apartment on the West Side, ostensibly to help with spaced-out Zeke, and instead had sat in Carl's bedroom when he was out and smelled his clothes. His odor to her was meadow-green, hummocky, and lustful as a satyr. She was uninterested in being around anyone else, and her friends began avoiding her. Her old boyfriend disgusted her with his unlikeness to Carl, and she was happy when he stopped calling and she heard he was with someone else.

Not having to work anymore, being able to go anywhere and do anything, meant startlingly little without the man she loved. She didn't know that Carl's alpha androstenol, which the eld skyle had fitted for Evoë, approximated the sex-cueing hormonal receptors deep in her own limbic brain. And she wouldn't have felt otherwise if she had known. Carl's mountain-valley scent had led her to the heart's edge, high above reason. There she lived for him, working out daily in the building's spa to keep toned, reading everything she could find in the libraries about black holes, and waiting.

She had not seen Carl in over a week the dawn he came to her bedroom. He was relieved she was not with someone else. He had been oblivious to her when she last came by Claremont Avenue to see him. He hadn't known Evoë was still alive then, and he was in a deathful mood. Afterward, he was sure he'd never see her again.

Zeke had grunted about the idiocy of hurting someone who knew as much as she did, but he didn't care. He had the lancer armor and the lynk, and he'd fend off the whole planet for the next twenty-two days if he had to. That arrogance was the numb callus of his soul. It shielded him from the pain of a life without Evoë. Now that he knew his mate was alive, he had become vulnerable again. He had someone to live for—and dying became frightening again.

Carl did not go to Sheelagh for sex, though the anxiety in his thews was erotic. The zōtl were coming to kill him, and Evoë was waiting for him not to fail. The tension of t rror and hope trilled in him with the same voltaic resonance as lust. The energy had floated him down Riverside, across Seventy-second Street, through Central Park, and east along Fifty-seventh Street to Sutton Place.

Zeke's speech had replayed in him several times, running on the charge from his tension, and he had decided to take what comfort he could in Sheelagh.

Sheelagh roused from sleep gently, cooed awake by subtle magnetic pulses from the lance tucked up the sleeve of Carl's sweater. The fragrance of sunridden grass rushed her awake, and she sat up surprised to find Carl beside her. "Carl!" Her red-blond hair was tangled in sleep curls, and when she lifted her arm to unsnaggle it, the bedsheet dropped enough for Carl to see the pale, ample curves of her breasts. "What are you doing here at this hour?"

"I've got to talk to somebody." Carl slid the lance out from his sleeve and held it in both hands across his lap. "I'm sorry to sneak in here like this. I should have waited in the TV room till you woke up. But the craziness of all this is zooming in. It's all too weird. I had to be with someone I trust. Zeke is just coming out of his chemical mixup, and your mom thinks I'm Satan's protégé. You're the only one I can turn to."

"Wait a minute." She hopped out of bed and capered naked to the bathroom.

Carl sprawled across the bed. He felt mischievous with desire—the first conscious lust he'd felt since losing Evoë. The Foke were not monogamous, and he knew Evoë would encourage him to be socially sexual while they were apart. The Werld, after all, had no venereal disease. The thought of her warmed his desire. At least she was alive. Only the zōtl and one hundred and thirty billion light years separated them, obstacles which seemed small beside the infinite abyss of death.

He moved to place the lance on the nightstand and noticed a book on gravity waves and cosmology. Sheelagh cared enough about him to want to learn about the universe that had changed him, and that insight sundered the desire in him. Why had he implicated this girl in his grotesque fate? Why had he come here this morning except to use her to counter his anxiety? He felt ashamed of his selfishness, and he was at the bedroom door, on the way out, when Sheelagh stepped back in from the bathroom.

172

"Please—don't go." In the chalky dawnlight, her nakedness glowed.

Carl paused in the doorway, awed by her lovesick body. His shame was slipping away like sleep. Her milkwhite breasts swayed with her advance, and he let his eyes drop to the garnet-yellow hair between her thighs. He closed the door, and they sat down on the bed together. She took the lance from him and laid it on the floor. The words he wanted to speak went breathless in him as she pulled off his sweater and unbuckled his pants.

He felt the hungriness of a cloud of mosquitoes in his loins, and as the last shred of restraint frayed, the light lancer armor inspirited a thought. Carl suppressed the chilly sensation of the other inside him. He had gotten good at ignoring the armor since he had found something like a no-time within himself. The Zone, as he called it, was a recess in his psyche where all the sounds, sights, odors, and textures of the day went within his head. With a little concentration, he could drop the armor's psychic intrusions there, too. All he wanted to know from the armor was when the zōtl had arrived for dinner. The white noise of the Zone smothered the armor's inspiriting, and Carl turned away from his farflung hopes and fears for the lubricious moment.

Sex was a lens of exhilaration, amplifying parts, like the shifting rococo of her hair on the pillow and her eyes like decorated glass, chromed with tears of joy as his hand fetched the lily of her genitals. His touch floated like a piece of light, and they twined together like music. He timed his deft massage to the green pulse of a vein in her throat and the rhythms of her breasts. Her song steepened and then frenzied as an orgasm bloomed through her. She clawed at the hand welded to her bluehot center and cried.

A scream cracked the tempo of her pleasure, and

she was rudely shoved aside as Carl bounded to his feet. "Hee-yipes!" he howled, clutching his hand. His face was skullwhite as he examined the hand and saw two thin wires of blood glinting from his knuckles to his wrist.

"What's the matter?" Sheelagh asked in a hurt voice. "It's just a scratch."

He faced her with a stare like an ax. "Oh, God," his huge face whispered. His wild eyes searched the room and fixed on the doily under the nightlamp. He ripped the doily from under it with such force that the lamp was dashed to smithereens. He clamped the cloth against his cut hand.

Sheelagh curled up with fright. "Carl, what's wrong? It's just a scratch."

He picked up his lance and aimed it at her. "Put out your hand. Hurry."

She balked, cringing with fear, and he grabbed her hand and irradiated it with UV. But the lance shut down before it would damage her.

Carl dropped the lance, bolted to the bathroom, banged around there, and burst into the laundry closet. When he lurched back into the bedroom, he was uncapping a jug of bleach. "Give me your hand," he ordered.

Sheelagh crawled into the corner. "What are you doing?"

"Just give me your hand, goddammit!" He was splashing bleach all over the bed, and when she hesitated, he seized her wrist and doused her whole arm in bleach. While she wept, he soaked her fingernails. Sweat beaded like mercury across his brow, and his face trembled.

"I'm sorry—I'm sorry," he mantrumed while he finished immersing her fingertips in palm-cupped bleach. Then he clambered into his clothes. "Stop crying—

please! It's not you. It has nothing to do with you. Do you understand?"

"No!" she blubbered.

"I have to get out of here." He backed toward the door.

"Don't go."

"I'll come back," he lied.

"You're lying. You're leaving for good. I'll never see you again. I know it."

"No. Don't talk like that," he said from the doorway. "But I've got to go now. Please—forgive me."

Sheelagh sat hunched over her tears in fearful confusion, and when Carl galloped out of the apartment and the door banged behind him, she collapsed under an avalanche of sobs.

Carl phoned Zeke from Ames, Iowa, and had him take the next flight out. The trip was Zeke's first time out in the world by himself in a long time. He dressed inconspicuously in loafers, gray slacks, blue shirt, bowtie, and tweed blazer. He was apprehensive about being recognized, and a fugitive anxiety accompanied him even in the privacy of the cab to the airport. His mind was clear, however, and he was pleased with how easily he flowed back into the stream of things.

A limo picked him up at the Des Moines airport and drove him through the long fluent miles of resinous land to a lonely warehouse big and empty as a ship's hull. Workers toiled with electric saws, hammers, and welders, fitting living quarters into a corner of the warehouse.

Carl met him at a scaffolded loading dock cluttered with lumber, fixtures, and pipes. They sauntered toward the warehouse under streamers of construction noise, and Carl told him about the spore.

Zeke went moth-white and fluttery. His eyes were

glazed brown fruits when they saw the bandage strapping Carl's hand. Carl explained about Sheelagh and him, and Zeke sat down on a stack of cinderblocks.

"You've known about this all along?" he asked in a shadowy voice. "Why did you come back?" The answer returned to him with the shock of a revelation: *Carl had never left.* His bodymind had journeyed among universes but his soul was everyone around him—all complicit with his betrayal of life on earth. A shudder twitched through him.

All Zeke could think to say was: "I can't believe you've had the balls to shave each morning."

Carl's contrite face brightened. "I don't. I use this." He lifted his left arm, and the red lens of the lance glinted from under his cuff.

Zeke experienced a warm flush on his cheeks and chin, and he looked down to see a fine dust of whiskers powdering his shirtfront. "*You're* the crazy one," he said, challenging Carl with the boldness of his stare.

"You're surprised at that?" Carl responded. "After all I've lost, you expect me to be sane?"

"Lost?" The veins in Zeke's temples drummed. He thought of slugging Carl, but knowledge of the spore dissuaded him. "You've got a perfect body, an armor with godful powers, and a lance that gives a great shave. What've you lost? Earth-one, a savage greed-confounded toxic dump? Evoë? Does she love you with more passion and more surrender than Sheelagh? Is she more beautiful?"

"It's not that."

"Damn right. What *have* you lost?"

"The ordinary." He dragged out a sigh. "It's strange now. I can barely remember when life was ordinary enough to be boring. I miss that."

"So you've endangered a whole world to recapture

a feeling?" Zeke thwacked his notebook across his knee and looked away.

"You're the one that believes the universe is infinite. What are you worried about? There are plenty of other earths, right? And besides, you're the one who told me to take my pleasure when I found it."

"That was before I knew you had parasites." Zeke stood up and looked about at the hustling workcrews. "What the hell is all this about?"

"It's a place for you to stay while the lynk converts you for the jump. We go in three weeks, but now it's too dangerous to stay in New York. So we're going to have to stay with the lynk."

"But the lynk is with the pigshit in Barlow."

"I'm moving it. Now that I've so handily charmed Sheelagh, I've got to cover our tracks. The dung and the lynk will arrive here tomorrow at the end of a trail of redtape that completely buries any tie between this place and Alfred Omega. I started the process weeks ago, after you told Dr. Blau who I was."

"That's the smartest thing you've done yet," Zeke muttered as a foreman approached Carl and presented an order sheet for his signature.

When they were alone again, Carl confessed: "It was the armor's idea."

"I should have known." Zeke's heart was erupting with feeling. The shock of what Carl had revealed mingled hotly with the gleeful expectation of the journey ahead. He felt gargoyled. "Perhaps Sheelagh won't go to the authorities. Maybe the spore wasn't released. It is just a scratch, right? And the armor hasn't imploded you."

"Sheelagh may be all right," Carl agreed. "But if I were her—"

"You mean, if the armor were her—"

"Yeah, it's the armor's belief that Sheelagh is going to turn us in. It's her only way of keeping me here."

"The armor's right. I asked Sheelagh once if she'd come with us. Her look would have poached an egg. She wants you, and she wants you here."

"But we're so close to getting away, Zeebo. I'm going to see if I can talk her out of interfering."

Zeke's face bobbed forward. "You're what?"

"I'm going to talk with her."

"You're not going back?"

"I want to see for myself if the authorities are on to us."

Zeke slapped his forehead as if suddenly comprehending. "Of course! And if they are?"

"Confront them." Carl pointed his left arm at a screwdriver on a workbench and it propellered into the air and stabbed a wind-gusting paper scrap to the plank wall of the storage shed. "I'll make a deal. We still have the trump cards."

"Yeah," Zeke concurred in a breath of awe that went flat. "For now."

Carl glanced up at the blue silence of the sky. "For now."

That night while Zeke slept in one of the mobile homes parked at the site, Carl stood outside and used his lance to magnetically stroke the sleep channels in his friend's brain. When he was sure that Zeke was slumbering deeply, he entered the trailer and went directly to Zeke's notebook. He opened it to the latest entry and by the scalloped light from his lance, he read:

"Carl called today from central Iowa. I've flown out of my past and am interfacing the future here in Ames. The old horror is over: My mind is clear again. But a new horror threatens. Carl carries the urg's spore. The whole planet is endangered by his presence. He is a

For all Zeke's mumbo-jumbo about light and infinity he was as intensely in this world as a mineral shard, and Carl felt unreal as a ghost. Nothing seemed as real as his memories of his lost life. The armor had him wholly in its grip.

"Look, I'm going to be on my way," Carl said.

"Okay, then." Zeke led him to the sliding door. They stood together for a while in the chilled and loamy air of the churned earth. The dark land furrowed away on all sides.

"Be easy with Sheelagh," Zeke advised. "And be ready for the unexpected. Okay?"

"You have any prescient dreams you've been holding out?"

"No, but I can feel the uneasiness of the armor. Four-space is murky up ahead. Keep alert."

Carl nodded, slapped Zeke on the shoulder. "If there's any trouble, stay close to the lynk. The lance has cued your molecules to pass through the field membrane. No one can reach you there."

Carl walked out into the field. His armor lightning-flashed, and he was gone.

That evening, after eating microwaved lasagna and watching a Lakers game on the giant TV, Zeke lay down on the waterbed under a skylight meshed with stars. In moments, he was asleep, flying across the dizzy space of a dream.

He saw the silverblue scimitar of the earth cutting the night, and the beryl sparks of Steel Wheel I and II, the cislunar factories, glinting in the span of emptiness between the earth and the lopsided moon.

The dreamflight pitched steeply, and all at once Zeke's awareness was mizzling in a sparse, modern apartment. Sheelagh and Carl were there before a window glittering with the constellations of the Manhattan skyline. He couldn't hear what they were saying at first, but he didn't need to. Sheelagh was undressing, her valentine-face mirthful as a mask. Her hair looked teased and her lispy mouth nervous. If she was hiding something, Carl didn't seem to notice. He was asking his armor if there were any threatening psyches nearby. The armor detected none.

Then sound swarmed over Zeke's ghost presence: "You loved me once," Sheelagh was saying in a voice like an empty seashell. She opened her wrinkled blouse and slinked off a sleeve.

"That was before Evoë," Carl answered, dryly. Sheelagh was fragrant as warm rain, but he was not going to be tempted. "Come off it, Sheelagh. I'm here because I know you blabbed on me."

Her features went slick with surprise. "I didn't."

"It's all right. I'm not angry."

"You're not?" Her lipsticked mouth looked petulant again.

"Why should I be?" Carl smacked the lance against his palm like a nightstick. "I'm leaving this rock as soon as the lynk can carry me, and nobody can stop me. I want you to tell them that. Make them understand—so no one tries to stop me."

"There's still time." Her face was moony with love in a halo of static-frizzed hair. "Stay with me. And talk with them yourself. Let them hear what they can ....ore you go."

"No, Sheelagh. I came back to see you, not them. I have to explain why I behaved so wildly with you the other night."

"Sit down and tell me." She put her hands on him to guide him toward a Morris chair, and two blue sparks snapped from her fingertips.

Carl's eyes went fish-round. He looked again at her hair and the wrinkled blouse clinging to her pale flesh.

"I wasn't thinking clearly," he said in a voice crispy with apprehension. "The zōtl had me freaked. And I just felt I had to be with you. I needed sympathy."

"Tell me about it." She steered him to the upholstered chair, and the smell of her was fresh as the browse of a summer shower. "Here, sit down."

"I got selfish," he continued through the static of his nervousness. "And, well, to get to the point—I think I exposed you to the same spore that first turned me into light. The spore's in my blood, and—"

"You what?" Her romantic mask curdled to a scowl.

"The euphoria you're feeling—the sparks..." His hands opened futilely before him. "They're all symptoms, Sheelagh! But you don't have to be afraid—"

"You infected me?" Anger and fear pulsed in her eyes. "I'm going to be taken to that other world?" Her breath spit with her shock. In a gesture made strong with her sudden loathing, she shoved Carl, and he dropped backward into the plump chair.

The springloaded hypodermic hidden in the cushion punched him squarely in the upper right quadrant of his buttocks, and his face buckled with shock. Zeke felt Carl's outrage as he realized he had been duped. He raised the lance at Sheelagh, and she gasped, the angry flush of her face draining to the color of metal. But the drug was a nervelock, and one second later, Carl was paralyzed. Another second, and he was unconscious.

Time collaged, and Zeke witnessed the arrival of the police and the siren-whirling transport of Carl's body to a surgery room in Sloan Kettering. The images shrank and went colorless, wrinkling up like a mushroom, collapsing into the dark duff of sleep.

Carl woke to a searing headache. His brain felt sunburned. When he opened his eyes, the blisters inside his skull winced with the weight of the light. He tried to sit up, but his muscles were so much cooked squid. The brash light sat on his chest, and his eyes adjusted enough for him to see that he was in a white-tiled observation chamber. An overhead camera silently watched him. His hands fluttered over his body, and he felt wires taped to his nakedness.

"Carl Schirmer," a woman's voice spoke. "I am Commander Leonard. You are in my charge now, and I've placed you under maximum security watch—for obvious reasons. Are you willing to cooperate with me?"

Carl squinted up at a whitehaired old lady with cheeks brown and wrinkled as walnuts. Her iguana eyes regarded him dispassionately.

"What've you done to me?" Carl groaned. He was hollowed out, and the gonging emptiness terrified him.

"Your weapons have been removed, Carl." The clack of a lock resounded in the chamber, and a hatch opened at the far end. A muscular fellow in a scarlet jumpsuit waited there.

"Can you sit up?" Commander Leonard asked.

"I don't think so."

"Let's try." She lifted his head and put an arm under his shoulders. With an unexpected strength, she sat him up, and his head pounded like a diesel. His within life was vaporous. The hymn-presence of the armor was gone. Only the sinuosities of his body, shivering with alarm, were real.

"Now I want you to stand up," she informed him.

He looked at her as though she had asked him to kill himself.

She pulled off the wires taped to his body, and he leaned his face into the shoulder of her white jacket. The purple odor there reminded him of the kindly matrons that came to St. Tim's on holidays to play with the children.

"We've taken the armoring chip out of your skull," she said, helping him to stand. "We couldn't take the chance of leaving it in. And even with it out, we've kept you unconscious just to be sure. You've been out for three days now, and in that time we've examined you and your artifacts thoroughly."

Carl wobbled, and the scarlet-suited bouncer who had stepped into the chamber steadied him. Commander Leonard unfolded a green hospital gown. While she dressed him, she spoke: "You have the chromosomes of a newborn—no chipping on any of the alleles, and the supercoiling of your genomes is tight as it gets. You're genetically perfect. And that means you're somehow artificial. You're not really human."

The pain in his head was dimming, and psychic space rippled like wind-bright curtains.

"The painkiller should be coming on about now," Commander Leonard said, fastening the gown's ties behind his back. "I think you can walk. Please, try."

He swayed forward, and the guard guided him. At the hatch, his escort put a hand on his head to keep him from braining himself as he went through. The outside of the chamber was darker and cooler. The guard led him down a melon-pale corridor past doorless office stalls. To one side was a burned-out cavity that had once been an office. The black, tar-droopy shapes of a desk and chairs were discernible in the ash-slush.

"That's where Sheelagh caught light," Commander Leonard's grandmotherly voice said. "No one really believed her story until that happened. Fortunately, the agent interviewing her fled when he saw green fire crawling over her."

"Sheelagh—" Carl's voice cracked. "I infected her."

"Yes, and two others in the apartment building you bought her have also caught light in the last two days."

Carl wanted to speak, to explain himself, but his mind was tenanted with grief. "I didn't want this to happen—" he managed lamely. The guard nudged him beyond the cindered room, and anguish turned in Carl like a sense. "I'm sorry—believe me."

"We believe everything now," the commander said. "That's why we've gotten you up."

They came to an open elevator. It closed behind them and with a barely perceptible hug silently carried them up. "Your actions have threatened all life on earth," Leonard spoke. "You're a selfish, thoughtless man, Carl, and you should be punished for what you've done. But for now, we need you. And maybe our need is punishment enough."

Terror bristled in him. "The zōtl."

The commander's lizard eyes nodded. "The lance has been calling for you. It started at midnight. Listen."

Carl heard it: a rumbling, inchoate as thunder.

The elevator stopped, the doors parted, and the thunder became a bellowing that forced hands over ears. The guard pushed Carl into the withering roar. The cacophony stopped instantly.

Carl looked around. He was in an amphitheater ringed with computer panels and viewscreens. The floor of the chamber was a maze of consoles. People in uniforms and lab suits were coming out of the sound-proofed siderooms where they had been waiting. At the center of the electronic labyrinth was a gray velvet pedestal on which lay the gold lance and the electricity-colored armoring chip. A technician in a green smock picked them up in surgery-gloved hands and began working his way through the maze to them.

The viewscreens came on, revealing a milky dawn

sky. Pins of cold light flashed on the monitor screen with the glinting swiftness of rapiers.

"Needlecraft," Carl clattered more than said.

"If you can't stop them," Commander Leonard said stiffly, "the spore you infected us with won't have its chance to kidnap us."

One of the screens displayed an array of missiles with makeshift warheads. Their exhaust fires redshadowed the sky as they crossed the space where the needlecraft had been moments before. "Radar—where are they?" the commander queried.

"They're not showing up on radar," the reply came.

The technician with the lance and the chip stood before them.

Commander Leonard looked into Carl sternly. "You're the criminal who caused all this evil. None of us wants you to have your power back. But you're the only hope of stopping this invasion. Do you want to help us?"

"Yes—I'll do anything to make up for what's happened." He bustled with sincerity.

"Turn around, Carl," the commander ordered. "Let's hope this works."

Carl couldn't believe it. They were giving his armor back to him. But *could* they? They weren't Rimstalkers. They were just desperate. Carl prayed with all his vital fibers and the hollowness they held, praying for connection. *Please, God—give it back to me. I won't trip up this time. Please!*

The gloved technician peeled off the thick bandage at the back of Carl's head and inserted the chip in the plastic-prised incision there.

Dazzling pain kicked Carl forward, and the guard holding him staggered. A red-blue spark jumped from the incision like a viper, and everyone stepped back.

Carl's headache wisped away. Colors seemed to go brighter. Space became translucent with energy. Something like a steel spring coiled tightly inside him, and the inspiriting began. The fires of his body gusted with the internal force of the armor, and when he turned about and faced the commander, he had the visage of a chieftain.

"Where are we?" the armor asked through him.

"At a missile-firing range on the tip of Long Island," Commander Leonard responded. She took the lance from the technicians and handed it to him. "We're a thousand feet underground. The elevator will take you out."

The touch of the lance quickened him with bright force, intoning the urgency of his mission with the drive to move. He strode into the elevator and jabbed the top button.

On the ride up, he caught himself in the gap between his feeble humanity and the armor's power. He felt like the muddy center of the universe. How had *he* come to this? He was Carl Schirmer, the avatar of ennui, the eternal ephebe, always more eager for ambience than destiny. He had never expected, much less asked, for his fate, least of all the ravishments of Evoë. It was losing her that had driven him mad. He was a false hero, a fool at the limits of reality. But his love for her was real. And he was thinking of her when the elevator stopped and the door opened.

Dawn gashed the sky. Carl settled into the embrace of his ribs, leaned back against his spine, and stepped out of the bunker onto the wide, saltgrass-tufted field. His armor came on, and like a piece of the sun, he lifted into the blue sky.

Needlecraft flitted in every direction, and the armor spun him, punching out with laserlight. The sky erupted with blue and green roses as each of the zōtl craft was hit. The rumble of their destruction zeroed in all directions. Carl circled about, waiting for more craft to come through the lynk.

The atmosphere above him limbed with a startling luminance, and a bulbous, spidery shape of gluey blue fire appeared overhead.

Carl wanted to fly off, but instead the armor lowered him to the rock-strewn range. The sandy ground was flat to a horizon rimmed with sand bluffs. The silverblue spider landed in a torrent of dusty light. And just looking at it, Carl knew the lance would be useless. This was Rimstalker armor fitted to a zōtl.

With grim resoluteness, Carl's armor stalked toward the fang-grinning abstraction, and Carl went brainless with fear.

The zōtl snapped forward. At the instant of contact, the two light lancer armors flashed with molten sparks. The armors grappled, and their tormented shapes flexed larger than life, quaked brightly, and disappeared.

Carl's bare feet stunned onto the rocky terrain, and the salt air gripped him. His rusty hair and the loose material of his hospital gown jumped with the clap of wind that followed the armor's shutdown. A stink of soured flesh slicked by, and he reeled backward at the sight of the unarmored zōtl that appeared before him. The male and female zōtl were not together. The bulging sac of the female was an arm's length away, the orange slug-mawed crown drooling its vomit stench as it gilled the planet's thin air.

Carl looked swiftly about for the male. It was hovering just behind him, and as he turned, it slashed forward. Its blade-curved beak gouged his scalp, and the hook-spurred legs dug into his face and neck. Carl beat the spidershape with his lance, and it sprang loose and jumped over him. He dodged instinctively, and the creature's sharp beak hacked the air just above his ear, its jabbering mouthparts flaying his scalp and chewing mad sounds in his ear. He batted it away and swung toward the barrelshaped female.

The male dove at Carl in a frenzied attack, cutting the flesh on his right hand and making him drop the lance. The jointed legs dexterously retrieved the lance and flung it away.

Carl tackled the female, pulling the thing over by the shocks of its ape-thick hide. It took him down with it, and the male's legs ripped into his shoulder while its feedtube desperately lanced at his throat, seeking the carotid. His right arm was pinned under the female's bulk and his left hand cramped with pain as it reached up and lay hold of the frantic sticklybacked thing.

The hot blood spilling over his face blinded him, and he squeezed shut his eyes and contorted the length of his body to avoid the spider's scissoring jaws and razored feedtube. With terror's adamant strength, he tore the zōtl from his flesh. He held the mad, writhing shape in his gory grip, away from his face, as he heaved the female over and freed his right arm. Its cries throbbed in the air.

Carl clenched a handy rock, the earth's first weapon, and pounded it into the spiderbeing. Spurts of black blood slapped him, and a haggard wail bawled from the female. It was rolling and twisting, spewing putrid ichor in long convulsive arcs. Carl picked up a flat, two-handed rock and used it to crush the zōtl. The work was ugly. The inside of his face was scalded with the sick smell, and the gash wounds on his body screamed with pain. The rock slab beat down hard on the split chiton and jumping viscera of the monster until his armor snapped on with a crack of lightning.

He recovered the lance and bathed himself with anesthetizing pulses. The armor directed the lance, and the wounds were sonically cleansed and cauterized. Miraculously, no tendons or major bloodways had been cut. Then with the sun spread out on the horizon like a red river, the armor lifted him and ricocheted him off the sky.

Ames, Iowa, was untouched. A few of the townspeople had seen needlecraft arrowing through the sky that night, but none had landed and none had been seen since. Carl's armor detected no zōtl activity anywhere. He was glad for the miles of unsullied land that surrounded Ames. He was sick from the zōtl killing and was grateful that no humans had been killed, including himself.

The sight of the lynk warehouse was a relief. Carl was sure it would have been a target, but the zōtl in the short time before his armor was returned had obviously never found it. He touched down before the partly open sliding door. His wounds were glossy, lacquered with the first sheen of scabs.

"Zeebo!" he called out as he entered. Beer-colored klieg lights gushed from the arched ceiling over the expansive interior. The living quarters looked lived-in: The giant TV was on, glowing with coverage of the worldwide UFO sightings. He turned the screen off. "Zee—where are you?"

Carl roamed through the kitchen and sleeping quarters to the back of the warehouse. The lynk field tingled over him as he approached the hill of tarp-covered pig dung. He rounded the far end of the mound and was frozen by what he saw.

A bloated human figure was bent over a zōtl female, face forward in its ooze-bubbling mouth. The male was clasping the back of the bruise-stained head. The body jerked upward and pivoted about. Through the blue-puffed features and the gangrenously swollen body, Carl recognized his friend. It was Zeke. The agonized eyes nailed him, and the turgid body careened forward.

Carl glimpsed a hip-high parabola of glassy metal—a lynk—before he dodged Zeke. A silvergreen light streamed through the parabola, which he could just see beyond the stout shape of the zōtl female. He fired an inertial pulse at it, and the barrel shape burst apart.

Before he could fire again, Zeke grabbed him. They struggled across the floor of the warehouse to the back wall. Zeke had Carl in a headlock, and Carl was hooking back with his legs, trying to trip him. He beat the lance against Zeke's sides, not wanting to fire on him. Their locked forms smashed against the back door of the building, and it burst open under the impact. They fell through, and Carl twisted out of the powerful grip and rolled to his feet.

Zeke was on his hands and knees, cumbersomely rising. Carl fired a carefully aimed pulse to the back of Zeke's head, and the zōtl spider fell away, its feedtube sliding out of the skull slick with blood chime.

Carl rolled Zeke over. The blue thick face was crazed, the eyes yellowed, unfocused. The lance magnetically soothed the brain and sheathed the body in a flux of vitalizing energy. Soon Zeke's gaze was focusing and his voice mouthing toward sound.

"Zōtl—lynk," Zeke rasped.

"I know," Carl reassured him. "I saw it. I'll go back in and destroy it."

Zeke clasped a black-fingernailed hand on his arm, his bruise-quilted face gasping to speak. Before he could, the air shocked to an icy brilliance. The warehouse was filled with an enormous light. The radiance seeped through the cracks of the walls and streamed in great beams out of the windows and the back door. Then darkness.

The armor filled Carl with understanding: The

zōtl lynk had inadvertently provided the necessary inertia to lynk the pig manure with the Werld—two weeks early. The armor also inspirited the news that unless he got himself into the warehouse within the next few minutes, while the lynk echoes were still strong, he would be unable to lynk at all. He would be permanently stranded on earth-two.

He peered down at Zeke, whose tormented face was relaxing toward the semblance of a smile. "Go—" he husked. He wanted to tell Carl so much—about the marvels of pain the zōtl had revealed—about the supernatural calm inside the emptiness of the spirit where only pain can go—but his mouth barely worked. "You—can't do—anything for me." His lips hooked toward a smile. "Go—"

Carl used the lance to radio for help. He made Zeke as comfortable as he could, laying him in pain-easing currents from the lance. If only he could take Zeke with him—but his friend's inertia belonged to earth-two, not the Werld. Carl's insides were jumping with the eagerness to go, but he still had to force himself to turn away from his friend. At the back door, he looked around and waved. Zeke's finger twitched. Carl walked into the warehouse.

A moment later, the door and windows flashed with a majestic fulgor. The darkness that settled back was salty with tiny lights for a long time afterward.

Carl appeared for a few seconds in Rataros. The black flames were frozen, still as megaliths, and in this pitch dark, the animal in him was close. He felt fear like a wetness inside him, cold and electrical. He was alone with that fear within the vacuum of himself. The armor had been taken away again.

Suddenly, horizons of red clouds appeared. Great strides of clouds! He tumbled into a gulf of skyles and cloudlanes, falling from lynk to lynk on his light-second-long journey to the eld skyle. The lance was still in his hand, and he clutched the weapon close to his body. He noticed then that he was garbed in a leather finsuit and strider sandals.

He was numb with the horror of losing Zeke, yet by the time the sky had brightened to the beaten bluegold luster of the Welkyn and the eld skyle's giant moss-veined walls were turning below him, awe had softened his feelings. The black waters of the eld skyle's lake gleamed deeply as opal.

He slid over a fallpath to the wall of the lake. Thornwings were everywhere, cruising low over the water and dropping in dark bales. As he climbed down the wall, he saw the mound of pig manure on the beach below him. Thornwings were gathering the dung and dispersing it on the waters. Among the slopes of dung were scattered articles from the warehouse: a chair, a houseplant, pots and pans, and Zeke's black-and-white-speckled notebook. He picked up the notebook and looked out over the lake, waiting for the eld skyle to speak.

Nothing happened. He waded into the lake and even immersed himself in the thick water. Still nothing. On shore, while he waited, he flipped through Zeke's journal. He read:

"Emptiness. Carl is gone. I'm alone. Really alone. The connection with the armor has vanished. For the first time in over two years, I am just myself again. No inspelling. No surges. Strangely enough, that doesn't bother me at all. In fact, I'm glad. I guess I've finally learned: A man must love his own to stay a man."

The gravel clacked behind Carl, and he jumped about with a shout. He saw a brown tangle of vines and vetch with a green scar glowing behind a fist-sized birdhead. The thornwing's stately walk stopped a pace away, and its tendriled arms lifted and opened.

"You've come for me, my old friend," Carl acknowledged. "Okay—we'll go." He looked out over the eld skyle's lake one more time. The other thornwings were still splashing bales of manure into the lake. Somewhere in its depths Sheelagh's strangeness was being digested. And others, too. Someday he might meet them. If he hadn't killed the eld skyle by overloading it. A pang of guilt cramped through him.

"Don't worry about me," he heard the eld skyle's voice, far, far within himself. He startled. When he strained to hear, it was gone. Then: "The spores you released were limited. Only eighty thousand or so people will catch light before the number of spores is exhausted. Their strangeness feeds me well. It pulls me away from you."

The eld skyle thinned off. Feebly, the voice returned, inside the ringing of his earbones: "But listen. Though the Rimstalkers have taken back their armor, they've left you the lance."

"Great," Carl grumped. "A sword and no shield."

"More than a sword," the shadow-thin voice said. "It is a bomb. When you pull off the hilt, it will trigger a starfire geyser that will cut off any approach—a wall of impenetrable energy. Use it to save your Evoë. The thornwing knows where to take you. That is all I can do for you—all that is left in me of you. Goodbye, Carl Schirmer. And glad fortune to you."

Silence hissed.

Carl smiled sadly and proudly. He saluted the eld skyle with his lance and stepped backward into the bristly embrace of the thornwing.

The thornwing carried him through several natural lynks, rolling down a fallpath in the intense, bluegold light of the Welkyn. The pure white and languorous clouds poured through the skyles on their endless spiral climb toward the shear winds of the Eld. Their gray velvet interiors blanked his thoughts, and he burned in the sliding silence with the power of his return. Zeke's notebook tucked into the back of his finsuit and the wounds from his zōtl fight were the emblems of his striving. And Evoë was at the end of this journey. The lance in his firm grip was cold. Its alien works clicked and purred. In the open spaces, Carl took shots at rock spires and treetips, remembering the use of the lance. It was difficult without the armor to help him select the lance function and to aim. Then they dove through the Cloudriver for a long time, and there was nothing to see. The emptiness jammed him toward sleep.

When the clouds burst apart, they were within sight of Galgul. The roots of Carl's blood flinched at the dark sight of the City of Pain. Cindered debris plumed the sky casting a gravelly black pall over the remaining zōtl spheres. And though this was the Welkyn, the light was dim and redlong.

The thornwing hauled Carl through one of the dusty flightlanes that unfurled in carbon-black arcs about the broken city. Galgul was bound in a knot of clogged sky cut by fallpaths. But in the interim since the gravity wave had ruptured these spheres, the fine dust had settled with the heavier mangled shards into ribboning bands outside the free lanes of the moving fallpaths, and the thornwing could skim over the charred litter toward the core of Galgul.

Needlecraft cruised among the plasteel debris, but they were no threat. The lance alerted him with tones to the approach of the zōtl, and the thornwing was able to move with the streams of detritus closer to the cracked-open sphere.

As the shattered spheres neared, Carl glimpsed

through the cumbering fields of shrapnel one sphere that gleamed. His eyes strained, and his heart pounded with the effort to discern what was ahead, but the rubble had become too dense. The fallpath ahead grinded with orbiting gravel. The thornwing's flight faltered and stopped. It could carry Carl no farther.

Carl thought of clearing a path with the lance, but nixed the idea when he realized the next moment that it would draw the zōtl to him. He would have to go on alone.

He reached out and took hold of a scorched boulder. The thornwing let him go, and he was left hanging on the edge of the fallpath with the other debris. His weight nudged the housesized boulder, and in the diminished gravity they began a slow rotation. The tumbleweed that was the thornwing rolled toward the clear flightlanes with a farewell squawk and banked out of sight.

Movement in the distant direction it flew caught Carl's eye. He scrambled against the spin of the big rock and climbed to the turning edge where he could see human figures galumphing over the choked edge of the fallpath. Black dust swarmed about them like a haze of flies. By their silhouettes against the luminous blue shadow of the Welkyn, he saw that they were Foke and that they wore the black strider tunics of a suicide squad.

They were approaching, and Carl bent down and walked in synchrony with the rock's movement, staying in one place, ready to drop out of sight. The group bounded through the smoky air close enough for him to see their faces. They were strained with flight, eager to cover distance.

Carl's focus locked on the blackbearded, gangster-grim face of the chief. It was Allin! The thornwing had carried Carl to Allin—by its own design or the eld

IN OTHER WORLDS

skyle's, Carl had no time to guess. Allin rushed by meters away.

Carl moved to join them, and that instant the sky convulsed with the compression of a big explosion. A trollish cry gulfed hearing, and Carl threw himself flat. A tiny sun ignited from where the Foke had come, lashing the space around it with hot flechettes of slag. A needlecraft had tripped the Foke's plastique bomb. The jumpship it had been escorting veered sharply to avoid colliding with the fireball. The needlecraft trailing the jumpship spotted the fleeing Foke and broke off to run them down. Laserfire twinkled from the attack ships and thumped the rocks around the Foke to fiery bullets.

Carl took aim with his lance and fired. A beam of soothing infrared streamed from the muzzle. He cursed and twisted the calibrated hilt until it clicked to the setting that he had learned was gravity-sheathed laser bursts. He aimed again, and the first two bursts caromed off floating debris. The third hit the lead needlecraft by accident when it rolled into an evasive run, and it billowed into green fire and black smoke. The other needlecraft pulled away.

Carl turned the lance's wavelength cylinder to its longest extreme—gravity waves—and set the lance to fire a tightly compacted charge. He aimed at the black shining nacelle of the jumpship in the pinpointed distance and fired. He missed by a thousand meters, but it didn't matter. The immense shockwave of the blast flipped the jumpship out of the clearing and into a steel-strewn fallpath. The shock of its eruption ignited the needlecraft that had swung back to protect the ship, and the gray sky flared.

Recoil from the shot pushed Carl backward off the boulder, and he sailed into sight of the Foke. They were cowering behind whatever protection they could find, expecting the bowshock of such a strong blast to sweep

200

over them. Carl knew from experience that the lance's gravity bursts were shaped to scatter perpendicular to the line of fire. He curled to slow his recoil and used his fins to set him down on a chunk of blistered plasteel overlooking the Foke.

"Why are you wearing a black tunic, Allin, if you're going to hide?" he called down to them.

"It's the dropping!" one of the band identified him.

Allin was too astonished to speak. He looked for the shockfront and saw far off the fire lickings where the jumpship and the needlecraft had been. He looked back at Carl agog.

"You came here to die," Carl spoke to the band. "And you'd be little more than seared meatballs now if I hadn't come along." He held up the lance and manipulated the hilt so that the muzzle flashed once with starpointed radiance. "The eld skyle and the Rimstalkers have given me this—a light lance. I want to use it to free the imprisoned Foke." He pointed the white-smoldering lance at the distant zōtl sphere. "Will you give me your lives?"

The Foke had floated out from their coveys, and they stared at Carl in his leather finsuit and scarred face with wonder-loud eyes. Allin pulled himself up beside Carl. The Foke's dark-coiled bangles were pulled back from a face fierce as a Comanche's. He looked at the lance and into Carl's broad stare.

"You've just paid me for the lives you lost," he said in his gritful voice. "I will attack Galgul with you. But not for you. I go to this death for our Foke."

He started to take off his holster, symbol of the band's leadership, and Carl stopped him. "You'll lead the squad," he told the Foke chief. "I'll keep the zōtl off us."

Allin agreed, and he put a hand on Carl's shoulder. "We'll die together."

"Who said anything about dying? I just want hit-and-run rescue." Carl looked down into the squad' ferine faces. "Nobody is going to get killed. Right? They stared back with the clarified power of animals He looked back to Allin: "You sure know how to pic them."

They flew a fallpath close to the floating heaps c cinders and jumped a ride on boulders big as streetcar to keep out of sight. When the boulders' gliding orbi about Galgul came within sight of the ruptured sphere they slipped off and tacked across the fallpath.

The city-sphere filled space like a murky grotto Diamond grains sparkled in its depths. Allin's spyglas revealed them to be tiers of glastic-encapsuled Foke Somewhere in there was Evoë. The lance was alread buzzing Carl's fingertips with her proximity, and b aiming it at the cavernous sphere, he could tactilely fee the level where she was located.

Allin pointed to a scattered flock of jumpships i the umber aura of the sphere. Their range of fire swep every approach to the structure. And inside the cordon the flightlanes twitched with needlecraft.

Carl nodded, visualizing his attack. He signed the Foke to lie low and adjusted the lance for rapid-fire gravity bursts. But the setting wouldn't hold. The lance didn't have that capacity. He would have to single-fire the bursts, which meant that if he rhythmed the attacl wrong, if even one jumpship escaped his barrage, they'c be frittered by laserfire.

Allin hung beside Carl in the cloud of clackin; rubble that circled Galgul, and he saw the problem There was no cover this close to the flightlanes. Plas tique and handguns were useless. The only thing to d was to scatter and wait for Carl to attack.

Carl looked overhead to see that the space for hi recoil was clear; then he sighted the lance on the

warming needlecraft below and fired. The force
of the discharge flung him outward, and he spun with
he bore of his flight and fired three more bursts in the
vicinity of the hovering jumpships.

The pounding roar of the first shot resounded from
inside the cracked-open sphere, and the nigrescent
space thudded with the rutilant explosions of needlecraft. The three other pulses hit in quick succession.
One of them banged into the horizon of the sphere and
gored a hole in it, clouting nearby jumpships with
molten fragments. One hit a jumpship broadside and
blasted it and the four around it into blazing dust. The
last missed entirely and boomed a long way off among
the circling scrag.

Two nearby jumpships were left unscathed and
they swiveled in the direction of the firing, scanning for
targets.

To draw their attention away from Carl, Allin
signaled his band to advance, and they dropped from
their balled-up coverts and slid along the fallpaths
curving down into Galgul.

Carl was a whip of arms and legs, still whirling
from the ungrounded recoils. Allin swooped over to
him and grappled him in a steadying bearhug.

One of the jumpships had spotted the band, and
the blue light of its laser cannon trembled along the
grinning seam of its prow. With Allin stabilizing him,
Carl aimed and fired again. The direct hit inflamed the
dust-shadowed sky.

Allin whooped with excitement.

An orange, searing bolt of laser light cut the air a
meter away, and he cried out again, in alarm. The
stormy smell of burned air billowed over them, and
Allin swung Carl about to face the jumpship that was
diving toward them. The craft was too close for a gravity
burst. Carl snapped the lance into laser mode, hot

IN OTHER WORLDS

enough to cut open atoms, and fired a steady stream o
white starfire. The beam hit the black metal hull in a
wincing flare of vaporizing plasteel, and the jumpshi
screamed and swooped toward them. Carl didn't flinch
and Allin held him tighter. The chief's eyes were bi
with alertness as he watched the black skin of the
jumpship peel away like burning wallpaper.

The wail of laser-slashed metal bowled them back
ward the instant before the jumpship's tormented hull
freight-trained by them, almost within reach. The dra
of the plummeting craft whipped Allin and Carl after it
and they toppled behind. Squealing with sparks and
smoke, the jumpship plunged toward Galgul and splat
tered into a firestrewn smear across the curve of the
metal horizon.

Carl flapped for balance, and Allin gripped him b
the collar and, straining every instinct from a lifetime
on the fallpath, tumbled, rolled, and sledded with Car
through the stinging smoke into the grotto of the frac
tured sphere.

The squad was watching them from the torn edg
of the massive stock chamber. A honeycomb of capsule
Foke dangled toward the interior of the sphere. Alli
jumped with Carl, and they tumbled onto the buckle
plasteel ledge. Carl swayed to his feet with the help o
several Foke and glanced around at the crystalface
shelves of inanimate figures. The weapon whined wit
the release-signal the Rimstalkers had programmed int
it.

Warming lights came on, lighting up the grotto
and all the capsules opened with a collective sigh.

"Allin!" Carl pulled the chief away from his amaze
ment at the sight of thousands of stirring Foke. "W
have to move quickly and get the Foke to the Cloudgate
The zōtl's whole army must be on the way by now.
won't be able to hold them off for long. Take them ou

204

that way." He pointed through the glowering embers of
the shattered jumpship cordon. "That'll keep this sphere
between us and the rest of Galgul."

"But that'll leave us wide open out there," Allin
complained. "We should travel along the edge of the
fallpaths."

"That'll take too long," Carl said. "You have to go
straight across the clearing. That's the fastest way to the
Gate. Don't worry about the zōtl. Leave them to me.
Just get the Foke moving."

Carl turned away from Allin and let the lance's
slow humming guide him in the direction of Evoë. She
was downward from where he was, and he scampered
over the warped surface of the ledge to the sinuous,
metal-coil scaffolding the zōtl used as catwalks. On the
way down, he looked across the bowl of opened sleepunits
and saw scattered skirmishes where zōtl guards with
lasers in their pincer grips were attempting to herd the
Foke. But the humans outnumbered the guards. From
the upper ledges, Allin and his group were lighting
naphthal flares to guide the crowds toward the nearest
jump points for the fallpaths.

The hum in Carl's lance led him onto a level
packed with Foke bustling to get out. He shouldered
his way in the direction the hum pointed until the
bobbing heads and unfamiliar faces suddenly hazed out
of focus around a coraline-stitched black robe hooding a
cat-angled face with wide graygreen eyes. Carl's blood
turned to electricity.

The next instant, Evoë saw Carl. Moments ago she
had been dreaming that she was old. In that dream, she
didn't know what was happening to her. She thought
she was sick; she had never felt such impuissance. The
desire for rest seethed in her. Then Carl's face appeared,
sweet as bread. They made love in a jasmine-fusky
grove. And when they were done, she was herself

again, lavish with energy. The dream had burst into the grim waking reality of Galgul. At first she thought the zōtl had come for her. But the chamber ceiling had been blown away, and she could see the nests of fire and coils of smoke from the battle. She emerged from her sleep capsule with a shivering heart and was shocked to see everyone moving. She moved with them, toward the torn-open wall of the sphere where Foke were waving flares. At the sight of Carl, her whole body pulsed. They shoved through the crowd toward each other and collided into an embrace that locked out the Werld.

"Carl," the spice of her breath whispered along his cheek. "I had the most wonderful dream of you. I knew you would come back for me."

Carl soaked up the ferny fragrance of her. This was the pearled moment he had lived for. The feel of Evoë against him was lustrous, and his heart warbled with jubilation. Everything that was driven in him yielded. He stopped. It was not even necessary to go on living, repeating the farewell. This was the tip of being. From here he reached out with his soul and felt the empty spirit, the vacant poise of everything. He could die here.

Tears welled in them to the very brink of their eyes. "Evoë—" He searched for some scrap of language to dress his naked feelings.

Screams and the scuffle of a fight pulled his attention from her. A zōtl guard was flying over the crowd, shooting its laser wildly. Carl fired from the hip and smashed the thing to a fireclot.

He took Evoë's arm, and they moved with the crowd toward the naphthal flares. Needlecraft slashed overhead, and he unloosed another gravity pulse, dropping this one deep into the sky so that the implosion would pull the needlecraft away from the sphere. The earnumbing thunder of the pulse roared hearing to a muffled, bulging silence, and the encroaching needle-craft went off like flashbulbs.

The peristalsis of the crowd squeezed them up a wobbly rampway to the melted-looking edge of the sphere. The jump point was before them, but Carl held back. He had to get everyone out to complete the symmetry of his joy. While Evoë used the naphthal flare to direct the crowds, Carl watched the ash-choked sky. The flightlanes lifting away from Galgul toward the Cloudgate beyond the rubble were crowded with Foke. Needlecraft occasionally darted in from over the horizon of the sphere to strafe the exodus, but Carl stabbed at them with laser bolts and brought some of them down.

After a while, the air attacks stopped. Allin had come down from the crest of the stock chamber, his body sparking with sweat. "We're all out," he announced.

Some dim explosions sounded from within the building. "Those are the plastique traps we set on the access ports. The zōtl are coming in from the back of this chamber. They'll have lasers."

Carl hugged Evoë. "Go with him," he told her. "I'll be right behind you."

"No." Her eyes were certain as a staring angel's. "I'm not leaving you again."

At the far end of the chamber, sparks flurried, and the wall crumbled like incandescent cheese. The opening writhed with the arachnid shapes of the zōtl, and spurs of crimson laserfire flicked across the chamber at them. One bright bolt scorched the ground nearby and skipped vaporing plasteel between Allin's legs. He stood firm, but his whole body grimaced, anticipating the fleshmelting impact of a laser bolt.

Carl gripped the hilt of the lance and twisted it through a tight series of clicks until it snapped off. A foam of purplesilver light frothed from the muzzle end of the lance, and Carl quickly placed the weapon on the ground. He grabbed Evoë, and with Allin they fled from the zōtl attack and the jumping clots of sight-cramping radiance.

In an eyeblink, the onrushing zōtl and the sharp, crisscrossing tracery of their laserfire vanished in a sheeting flow of white incineration that nothinged everything before it.

Allin led the jump to the fallpath. Evoë and Carl leaped after him, hand in hand. They fell through a wind-flapping drop before the fallpath lifted them like a song above the char and the billows of killing smoke. Behind them, the lance squandered matter to light, and the zōtl sphere blustered with white fire. Ahead, the Foke rose out of the ruins on slants of light.

Carl and Evoë clamped their bodies together and sweeled away from Galgul, riding the steep current of a fallpath outward toward flamboyant cloud gorges iridescent with rain.

Epilog

Caitlin, with her grizzled hair hanging over her small shoulders, hooding the ruddy woodgrain of her face, stood at the glass-paned door. She was staring across the patio at the gazebo where Zeke sat motionless in a rocker, watching pillars of rain move across the wide lawns. Stormlight shone slantwise through the aspen, illuminating tall hedgerows powdered with mist. Several months ago, she and Zeke had been brought to this estate on Long Island by the government. There were seventy-two of them then, people with the highest chance of catching light. There were twenty-six now.

At the first letup in the rain, Caitlin opened the door and walked across the glossy flagstones and the sequined grass to the gazebo. Zeke didn't budge his stare from the sky, where the clouds were hitting a cold front and shredding like galactic vapors. His beard and hair had grown back in white goat tufts, and his former bulk had thinned to a skeletal frame. The zōtl clawmarks on his face and neck had faded to smoky bruises in his pale flesh like striations floating in marble.

"Two people in Maryland and one in Vermont have caught light," she reported, sitting herself in the rocker beside him. "The spores can't be contained."

Since their internment, Caitlin had been coming to Zeke, hoping to get from him some hope for her daughter. Instead, she had found peace, the humbling of life to memory and perception when all hope is lost.

"Gentleness and love will survive," Zeke spoke, his voice swollen with silence. He didn't care about the world's plight. The remorseless agony of his zōtl possession had purged him of all caring. Pain and pleasure had become for him two ends of the same board, the flimsy plank of his body, floating on a sea of electrons, riding the long currents of time to wherever. He felt more clarity than any man alive.

"What are you thinking?" Caitlin asked. The storm had frenzied again, and needles of rain prickled her skin.

"Why do people think heaven is up?" he replied. "I mean, look at it. The sky is tearing itself apart. I wouldn't want to go up right now."

Caitlin grinned at that thought and turned her attention to the wheeling sky. She hadn't had a drink since she was brought here, yet at that moment power was flushing through her like a shot of whiskey. The drugs that controlled her tremors usually left her dense with torpor. Now, watching the storm clouds stampeding like white bison, she was exhilarated: Something was going to happen.

"I'm leaving soon myself," Zeke said at last, and when his thin black eyes touched hers, she saw the happiness in his harrowed face. His short hair was bristly, and the blue regulation fatigues they both wore

210

looked wrinkled and ill-fitting. She reached out to touch his mottled hand, and a spark cracked between them. A gasp hissed through her lips.

"You want it?" he asked.

"Yes," the old woman answered.

Zeke peeled off a splinter from the arm of his rocker and lanced his left thumb. He offered her his hand and its gem of blood.

Caitlin's forefinger smeared the blood when a spark jumped to it from his thumb. She brought her finger to her mouth, and the taste of iron chilled her.

That evening, one of the residents complained that Zeke was glowing. Guards in bright-orange jumpsuits, hooded goggles, and gasmasks found Zeke in the gazebo grinning with muscular ecstasy. They took him to a protective chamber monitored only by cameras. He wrote a note to Caitlin, and fifteen minutes later, he caught light and vanished.

Caitlin received the note the next morning at breakfast. Even among the sinuous fragrances of coffee and toast, she could still smell the blue scent of a windshaken mountaintop on the paper. It read—

Caity—

What goes up
is futile—
unless it goes out.

—Z

From the author of
IN OTHER WORLDS
"An instant classic."
—*Washington Post Book World*

RADIX
by A. A. Attanasio

A Nebula Award finalist, RADIX is a brilliantly
realized vision of the future, so richly detailed
and convincingly imagined that it has won fa-
vorable comparisons to Tolkien's LORD OF THE
RINGS and Frank Herbert's DUNE novels. The
awe-inspiring tale of a young man's journey of
self-discovery from a life on the streets to near-
godhood, it is an epic of the highest order.

Buy RADIX, available wherever Bantam Spectra
Books are sold, or use the handy coupon below
for ordering: